What Willie suffered happened decades ago, his disappearance never solved, so why was Tobias dreaming about it now?

Vernita looked past her plate of eggs, grits, and ham. To one side of her, a woman shoveled food into her mouth, not looking away from her plate. At the other end of the table, an aide fed another woman.

"Open up," the aide instructed before placing a spoon with a small amount of applesauce into the woman's mouth. "Good. That's good."

Vernita clenched her fists, gritted her teeth, and began breathing heavily. She abruptly stood and glanced across the cafeteria. Then she knocked the items off her tray unto the floor. "He ain't coming back!" she screamed. "They kilt my son! They kilt Wilfred!"

Several aides rushed over and wrestled her to the ground. One of the aides signaled for a strait jacket.

Decades after migrating north to Cleveland, Ohio, from rural Louisiana, Tobias Winslow has made an uneasy peace with the past, including his own mistakes that led to a prison stint, and has found a way to thrive in the inner city. News of a murdered son, and the daughter that son left behind, forces Tobias to reassess his past and restructure his plans for the future. Christian Taylor and Joey Breaux, meanwhile, are students at a Cleveland-area historically black university who have vastly different worldviews, but are drawn together by an appreciation of family and, ultimately, a senseless, violent act. All three—Tobias, Christian, and Joey—are unknowingly tied together by a racially motivated killing in Louisiana decades earlier.

KUDOS for *Wilfred's Dream*

In *Wilfred's Dream* by Mark R. Lowery, Wilfred Foster disappears in 1964, and his disappearance was never solved. His kin and descendants have fought long and hard to bring justice for him, but to no avail. Now in 2017, Tobias Winslow, one of Wilfred's distant kin, gets drawn into the fight, becoming a "Wilfred's Dreamer," almost inadvertently. Tobias owns a barbershop in Cleveland, Ohio. He takes his aging and dementia-afflicted aunt to the Dreamer's gatherings, and thus becoming a Dreamer by "association." Then Tobias discovers he had a son, whom he never knew about, but the boy has been murdered, leaving behind a young daughter who seems to have no family other than Tobias, turning his life upside down. Well written, fast paced, and poignant, the story is thought-provoking as well as intriguing—a definite must read. ~ *Taylor Jones, The Review Team of Taylor Jones & Regan Murphy*

Wilfred's Dream by Mark R. Lowery is the story of bigotry, family pride, and revenge. In 1964, Wilfred Foster disappears and is presumed murdered. It is a crime that still remains unsolved in 2017. Because Wilfred was black and lived in the Deep South, his family believes that the police did not try very hard to solve the crime. His extended family has formed an organization called Wilfred's Dreamers, and they meet regularly, trying to bring pressure on the justice department to solve Wilfred's murder. Tobias Winslow, a member of

Wilfred's extended family owns a barbershop in Cleveland, Ohio, and takes his aging aunt, who can barely remember his name, to the local Dreamer gatherings, getting drawn into the Dreamers almost against his will. Then Tobias's world gets turned on its ear when he discovers that, not only did he have a son who was recently murdered, he has a granddaughter now with no parents and no place to go but to Tobias. Thought provoking, intense, and deeply moving, I think Wilfred's Dream is a book everyone should read. ~ *Regan Murphy, The Review Team of Taylor Jones & Regan Murphy*

ACKNOWLEDGMENTS

Thank you to the entire team at Black Opal Books. I'm proud to be part of your family. Special thanks to Anthony Mattero for his help in the development of this novel.

Wilfred's Dream

Mark R. Lowery

A Black Opal Books Publication

GENRE: AFRICAN-AMERICAN FICTION/SUSPENSE

This is a work of fiction. Names, places, characters and incidents are either the product of the author's imagination or are used fictitiously, and any resemblance to any actual persons, living or dead, businesses, organizations, events or locales is entirely coincidental. All trademarks, service marks, registered trademarks, and registered service marks are the property of their respective owners and are used herein for identification purposes only. The publisher does not have any control over or assume any responsibility for author or third-party websites or their contents.

DEDICATION

With love to my grandfather, Russell Lowery.
You deserved much more than your country provided.

Chapter 1

Vidalia, Louisiana, 1964:

A strong breeze from the Mississippi River dominated the July night, planting a fishy smell on everything within reasonable distance and launching small, flying pests everywhere, including onto Wilfred Foster's blue and beige 1958 Buick. Still, no one emerged from the Dew Drop Inn.

"C'mon, man," he mumbled to himself, glancing at his watch as he stood outside the bar. "C'mon."

He didn't want to go inside. Black folks weren't welcomed at this establishment. But if his client didn't emerge soon, Wilfred wouldn't be able to complete the rest of the work chores he needed to finish before the end of the day. With reluctance, he walked slowly toward the bar's entrance, pausing to steady his nerves. He walked through the door and took a single step before a burly man with a handlebar mustache and a motorcycle tattooed on one bicep halted his progress.

"Got business here, nigger?"

Willie scanned the room before answering, making eye contact with the man behind the bar. "I'm here to pick up Mr. Thornton," he announced aloud. "I was asked to take him to the Cloverleaf." He stared at the large man blocking his path. "Ain't looking for no trouble, Jimmy."

The bartender pointed to a lone patron near the back of the bar.

Jimmy slowly backed away from Willie without taking his eyes off him. The bartender snickered.

"Ought not to get involved in 'em nigger card games if you don't want to lose money, Jimmy," the bartender gloated. "Told you not to."

"I'll have the last laugh," Jimmy promised. "Wait and see."

Willie moved rapidly toward the diner. "Mr. Thornton?" he asked upon reaching him.

"Who wants to know?"

"Wilfred Foster," he answered, extending his hand. "Friends call me Willie. I was sent here to give you a ride to the Cloverleaf."

"The Cloverleaf?"

"For your appointment with Miss Missy."

The bartender smiled.

"Oh, yeah," Thornton replied. "My appointment. Don't want to miss that."

"My car's out front," Willie continued. "If we hurry, we can get to your appointment while your time is still available. I can't make any promises if we don't leave now."

Thornton placed a few bills on the table and followed Willie outside. As Willie held the car's passenger door open, Thornton removed his straw hat, adjusted his suit pants, and then sat down in the car.

"How long you say it'll take, boy?"

"A few minutes, sir," Willie answered. "Not long at all."

Willie started his car and turned on the radio. Jackie Wilson was in mid-song.

Thornton smiled. "Ain't nothin' like that jig-a-boo music. Nothin' like it."

When they arrived at the motel, Willie parked outside a two-story row of rooms. "Did you have something for me, Mr. Thornton?" he asked.

"Huh?"

"The envelope?"

"Oh, yeah," Thornton said.

He reached inside his jacket and pulled out a white envelope. Willie took it and peered inside.

"Miss Missy's waiting for you in Room Two-Twenty-Three. Right up them steps and to the left."

Thornton excited the car and headed to the steps. Willie drove to the motel office, parked outside, and then headed in. He handed the envelope to the manager behind the counter and then turned to leave.

"Willie," the manager called out.

"Yes, Mr. Caigny."

"Do you like your job, boy?"

"Why yes, Mr. Caigny," Willie answered. "Why would you ask that, sir?"

Caigny eyed the sign outside. Above a brick column, a green clover leaf rested above the words Cloverleaf Motel. Below it, on separate rows, were the words "air-conditioned," "telephones," and "vacancies." The "t" in "motel" looked like a lowercase "i," as some of the bulbs had burned out.

"Sir, I'm sorry," Willie offered. "I'm sorry. Got caught up at the bar waiting for a customer and didn't get to that. I'll fix it right now."

"No, no," Caigny said. "Tomorrow morning will be fine. Just remember, I've got plenty of young men looking for work. Gave you this job as a favor to your momma, Vernita. Don't make me regret it, boy."

"I do appreciate that," Willie assured him. "And I'll take care of that first thing in the morning. You have my word, sir."

Caigny handed three envelopes to Willie.

"Deliver these, and then go pick up Mr. Sam from his office," he instructed.

"Yes, sir," Willie answered. "Right away."

Written on each envelope was the number of the room to which it needed to be delivered. Willie knocked on Room 40 and waited. After a few moments, he heard the chain on the door being removed. A tall, strawberry-blonde emerged, peering out the door from under a large cowboy hat.

"Evening, Billie Joe," he said, handing her one of the envelopes.

"Thanks," she replied.

He heard another woman's voice inside the room.

"That Trisha?" he inquired.

Before Billie Joe could answer, a chubby woman with curlers in her hair appeared at the door. Willie gave her the second envelope.

"Thanks," she said.

No one answered the door at Room 67, but Willie could hear the television playing and water running in the bathroom. He assumed Betty was busy with a customer. He was walking away from the room when the door opened slightly, and Betty summoned him back.

"I have something for you," he announced, poking his head into her room.

Betty sat in front of a mirror combing her hair and checking her makeup.

"Put it over there," she directed, softly. "On the nightstand."

He dropped the envelope near the lamp and then turned to find Betty standing between him and the door. She was wearing an oversized shirt that barely covered her underwear. Her straight hair rested just above her shoulders. Walking to him, she gently ran one of her hands down the side of his face.

"What's your hurry, smooth?" she asked. "I do love me some fudge. Seems like every time I see you these days, you in a hurry. Trying to tell me something?"

He eased her hand away. "Working three jobs," he pointed out. "That's all. At times, I can't tell whether I'm coming or going. Got to do what I got to do though. Sure you understand."

She unbuttoned the top of her shirt and leaned toward him. "Maybe it's time to take a break," she whispered. "Let Miss Betty make you feel good all over. Spend a little of that hard-earned cash here."

"Can't do that," he retorted, gently pushing away.

"You sure?" she asked, slightly opening her shirt. "You ain't had no complaints the last couple times. Couldn't seem to get enough as I recall."

She pressed her lips softly against his cheek. He caressed her smooth shoulders momentarily.

"That can't happen again," he warned.

"Why not?"

"People talk," he muttered. "Folks 'round here don't take kindly to race mixing."

"How folks 'round here gonna know 'bout our business?" she asked. "You telling folks?"

"Ain't just that, Betty. I'm engaged now," he informed her. "Saving my money so Addison and I can get married."

She laughed. "Is that your dream, Willie?" she asked. "Marry some black Southern belle, buy some shack in the Colored section, and live happily ever after? Like in them books in school?"

He pushed past her. "Ain't planning on staying 'round here any longer than I have to," he insisted. "Gonna move north. To one of those cities with factory jobs. Milwaukee, Chicago, perhaps Cleveland. Got a cousin up there who told me there's plenty of work for anyone who can get there. And they hire blacks."

"Let me tell you something, smooth," she said, smiling. "I ain't been to any of them cities up north you mentioned. But I have been to Washington, Baltimore, and Philly. Dealt with plenty of men, both black and white. Do you know what those white men in those factories call black men?"

"No, Betty. Reckon I don't."

"Niggers," she replied. "Just not always to their faces."

He closed the room door as he left. Across the way, at the diner attached to the motel, two men watched intently as Willie left the room.

"That coon got some pretty big britches," one of the men said.

∽∾∽

On the back road into town, Willie's Buick created a sizeable dust trail that prevented him from seeing anything out of his rearview mirror. So, it wasn't until the driver of the unmarked police vehicle leaned on his horn twice and turned on his flashing light that Willie noticed him and slowed down.

He pulled his car onto the shoulder of the road and watched the officer through the rearview mirror. The officer exited his vehicle and circled the Buick, raising his dark sunglasses slightly as he did.

"License," the officer demanded.

"Is there a problem, sir?" Willie asked.

"Shut up, boy!" the officer demanded. "Did I ask you to speak?"

The officer snatched Willie's license from his hand and walked back to his vehicle. Willie lifted his eyes to the rearview mirror and watched the officer speaking into a police radio. After a few moments, the officer exited his vehicle and walked back toward the Buick. As he did, another car carrying three men pulled behind the officer's car.

"Get out," the officer demanded.

Willie tried to face the officer as he stepped out of his car, but the officer violently forced his head in the other direction.

"Walk to the front of the car," the officer instructed. "And keep your hands up where I can see them."

Again, Willie tried to turn and face the officer, but one of the men from the second vehicle struck him on the side of his face with a baseball bat before he could. A second man took another bat to Willie's kneecap, forcing him the ground.

Chapter 2

Cleveland, Ohio, 2017:

U n-cle Tom! Un-cle Tom! Un-cle Tom!"
Dozens of protesters—mostly students—stood near a terminal exit at Hopkins Airport, held in place by armed police away from the escalators to and from the airport's second level and the baggage claim area. One of their signs read *Supreme Knightmare*. Another read *Go back to Georgia*. Others unfurled banners on which Supreme Court Justice Harold Bilton's face was displayed atop a lawn jockey or donning a handkerchief similar to those once worn by Southern black mammies.

Joey Breaux stood on the other side of the police line, looking nervously at the protesters and then at the flight-arrival board. She'd considered it an honor when her pre-law professor at Frederick Douglass University selected her to meet the justice at the airport and accompany him back to the university, and she hoped that the police could shield him from some of the ugliness that began to mushroom on campus following the announcement of his visit. Most of the demonstrations were organized by professional protesters who had linked with left-leaning student groups to provide a visual presence at each of the justice's stops. A television reporter standing next to Joey answered her unspoken question.

"Flight Two-Zero-Five-Seven has landed," the reporter announced to no one in particular. "The show's about to begin."

Joey checked her lipstick and makeup in a small, round mirror, and then tucked it back into her purse. On the airport's second level, looking down on the scene below, Tobias Winslow sipped a beer inside a concourse restaurant and glanced longingly at the cigarettes in his jacket.

He closed his eyes and took several deep breaths, trying to prepare himself for the awkward conversation he was about to have. He hadn't come to grips with what the social worker had told him on the telephone. Was it possible he could have a son?

Down the concourse, moving toward Tobias, a well-dressed man surrounded by other, more official-looking men in dark suits made his way toward the escalator to baggage claim. The lackeys surrounding him carried mobile radios and glanced in each direction as they proceeded down the concourse.

"What's that about?" Tobias asked, looking at his server.

"The supreme court justice," she replied.

"Huh?"

"The black judge who's against affirmative action."

Tobias couldn't distinguish one justice from another—or any political leaning any held. The Supreme Court and the battles waged there couldn't have been any further from his world.

"Oh," he responded.

Downstairs, Christian Taylor directed the demonstrators.

"Let's go," he said. "Here he comes."

A senior at FDU, Christian had spent his first three years at the university seeking career direction. Other than a summer job doing community organizing, nothing he'd been involved with at the university had excited him or got his blood flowing as much as this demonstration. He felt he had to be at the airport.

As a sign of disrespect, the protesters closest to the police turned their backs to Justice Bilton as he approached. Then, in unison, they began backing their way toward the escalator, forcing the police line back as they did.

"Un-cle Tom!" they shouted. "Un-cle Tom!"

Joey walked to the bottom of the escalator to greet Justice Bilton. An officer escorted her while another directed people away from the exit door leading to the judge's waiting limousine.

Joey extended her hand as the justice reached her.

"Justice Bilton, I'm Joey Breaux," she announced. "I'll be accompanying you on your ride to Douglass University."

"Nice to meet you, Ms. Breaux," he said. "Thank you for meeting me."

"The limo's right outside," Joey informed him, over the roar of the protesters. "Do you have any baggage you need to retrieve?"

"Security will take care of that," he said. "We can go directly to the car."

She nodded, standing between Justice Bilton and the police line as the protesters inched forward.

"Go back to Georgia!" they shouted. "Go back to Georgia!"

Before she and Justice Bilton reached the exit, the protesters penetrated the police barrier, forcing Christian and one of the officers to fall forward and accidentally knock Joey to the floor. With cameras flashing, she glared wordlessly at Christian as a security guard helped her up. The security detail then whisked her and Justice Bilton out of the airport and into the limo.

Chapter 3

The vibrancy and rancor that had engulfed the airport evaporated swiftly as the justice left. The protesters took their traveling show to the university, some of the media followed, while other reporters and photographers hurried off to their next assignments, and airport workers moved about normally again. Tobias sat across from the young social worker he'd just met in person and tried to make sense of what she was explaining.

"Perhaps there's a better place to have such a sensitive conversation?" she suggested.

Tobias didn't immediately respond to the social worker's suggestion. Instead, he pulled a barstool out, directed her to take a seat with one hand, and then rested his corduroy Kangol cap on the counter. A motorized cart racing and beeping down the concourse momentarily diverted his attention.

"This is as good a place as any, Mrs. Brennan," he said.

"Call me Donna."

She retrieved a file from one of her carry-on bags.

"Well, Donna, as I told you on the phone, I think you're barking up the wrong tree," Tobias opined. "Really don't see how it's possible. I mean, how can a man have a grandchild 'fore you even have a child?"

She directed a wayward strand of her long black hair extensions around her ear. "I'm here trying to find the truth," she responded. "To do what's in the best interest of the child—wherever that takes me."

"So tell me again 'bout this young man," Tobias requested. "The one you think might be my son."

She placed a photo of the young man in front of Tobias. He shuddered involuntarily, feeling a chill run through his body as he eyed it. The man definitely had his nose—narrow at the top and broad at the bottom—his same small ears and long, dark hands. Anyone could see that.

"Elton Davis," she said. "About three months ago, he was killed during a home invasion in Los Angeles. Police found an eleven-year-old girl hiding in a closet when they arrived at the scene. Probably would have been killed too if the robbers had seen her."

"Sad," Tobias concluded. "Wish I could say I hadn't heard that story before. Get you a drink?"

"No thanks."

"They arrest anyone?"

"No. Elton sold drugs, so there were countless people who knew he had money *and* drugs. Doesn't exactly lend itself to a short suspect list."

He slid the photo back to her. "I'm still not seeing my connection to any of this."

"Lakisha, the girl, has been placed in a foster home while we search for her family. Turns out her mother is doing ten to fifteen in the pen. No other family we could identify on her side—at least not anyone suitable for a placement. Elton was an only child. His mother is dead, so that has us looking for his father."

She handed him another photo.

"Did you know a Kendall Davis?"

He put on his reading glasses and examined the photo. "Kendall?" he asked. "Name's not ringing any bells."

"Lived in Euclid," she interjected, looking down at her notes. "Says here she worked at Malcolm's."

"Malcolm's," he said, smiling. "You weren't even born the last time anything was served at that place."

"So Malcolm's is familiar?"

"Yeah," he admitted. "Used to work there. Right up 'til I caught a case."

She looked up from her files. "A case?"

"Long story," he remarked. "Don't remember any Kendall though."

"Worked as a barmaid. Says here she went by Sugar."

He reached out his hand and steadied himself with the counter. He began to feel faint. "You say Sugar?"

"Yes. You remember a Sugar?"

"Well, sort of," he recalled. "She was one of the women who hung out at Malcolm's."

"Did you date?"

He smirked. "Dating would be too strong a word. We hooked up a few times, as the young folks would say," he recounted. "Nothing serious. She had a man—the guy who owned the place."

"So it's possible?"

"It's not *impossible*. But how would I not know about a child?"

She put the photo away. "First thing we need to do is a DNA test. And while we wait for the lab results, I can learn a little more about your story."

"My story? Why do you need my story?"

"If you're the grandfather, then we'll need to determine if you would be a suitable placement."

"Placement for what?"

"Lakisha, the girl," she said. "That's why I'm here. To find her a suitable home."

Chapter 4

The leaves that remained on the trees fought hard against the wind but were losing the battle, falling rapidly onto the highway and the fields and lawns dotting the rural landscape. The strong winds also shook the justice's limo as it sped to the university. As Joey's body sank into her seat, it was difficult for her to determine where her body ended and the soft leather interior in the limo began. The interior of the limo was nicer than the interior of any place she had ever lived—and better equipped. She fought the urge to turn on the television in the limo or to fiddle with the laptop computer on the tray in front of her. Justice Bilton poured himself a drink.

"It should be about forty minutes to the university," the driver announced. "We should be there in no time."

Bilton turned to Joey. "Sure you don't want anything?" he asked.

"No thanks," she answered. "But I would like to apologize."

"For what?"

"That ugly scene back at the airport. Those folks don't represent the majority of us at Frederick Douglass University."

"No need to apologize," he declared. "Sort of comes with the territory. Your university's namesake once said, 'I'll join with anyone to do right—'"

"But with no one to do wrong," Joey interrupted, finishing the quote.

Bilton smiled. "The first part of that is easy," he explained. "It's the second part that takes conviction. And sometimes brings scorn."

"Don't quite understand your point, Justice."

"Telling people what they *want* to hear, especially when it's not what they *need* to hear—that's wrong. Everybody's happy when someone else is supplying their needs. Ask them to fend for themselves, and you've got a fight on your hands."

"You mean affirmative action?"

"You said that, not me," he mused. "But let's use that as an example." He topped off his drink. "At what point should it end? Should your children's children's children be given special treatment? Special status? At what point do we demand that everyone be treated equally, legally?"

"Justice, I sincerely hope my children won't need it," Joey retorted. "I hope they'll be living in a society that values everyone's contribution."

"Young lady, we're never going to live in a perfect society. But that doesn't remove personal responsibility to do all one can do to improve his or her own plight. People like Frederick Douglass weren't fighting for special treatment. They were fighting for a level playing field. Level the playing field, and I'll do the rest."

"Surely you acknowledge there are barriers that keep some people from succeeding. Your own story—at least what I've read—is one of someone who has worked twice as hard, run twice as far."

"I've got to get you to co-write my next book," he said, smiling. "There are barriers, you're right. Some are historical. Some are legal. Some are social. More and more are self-imposed."

Chapter 5

Tobias leaned against the front of his black SUV, puffing away at a cigarette. Donna sat in the front passenger seat, staring at the two-story building directly across the street. Its exterior was covered with light brown painted brick, the second story separated by a small, wood-shingled overhang. A neon sign shaped like an arrow pointed to the front entrance.

"Is there a reason we're here?" Donna asked, emerging from the car.

Tobias blew cigarette smoke into the air then looked toward the abandoned building.

"Said you wanted to know my story," he reminded her, pointing across the street. "That there is Malcolm's."

She diverted her eyes from him to the arrow sign that read "Galaxy Club."

He took another puff. "'Fore it was the Galaxy Club, and whatever it was 'fore that, it was Malcolm's," he explained. "Part of that salvage yard next to it was the park-ing lot."

"You were raised in this area?"

"Not exactly. We moved up here from the bayou. Louisiana. Was in the sixth grade when Mom and I came." He nodded his head northward. "Stayed 'bout a mile away from here in some friend's basement 'til we got our own place. Two-bedroom off Quincy."

"Was it just you and your mother?"

"Yeah."

"Why did your mother leave Louisiana?"

"Wasn't no reason to stay," he quipped. "Black folks, least those who could, were leaving fast as they could."

"Coming north for the jobs in the factories?"

"That was part of it," he acknowledged. "Those were the so-called pre-civil rights days. Black folks were get-ting all kinds of legal rights. The right to go in the front door of the restaurant, the right to vote. Problem was when you tried to exercise those rights."

He extended his pack of cigarettes toward her.

"Don't smoke," she noted.

"Lynchings, murders, disappearances, fire bomb-ings," he continued. "Just cause someone said you could do something didn't mean you could. Not like there was anyone to protect us." He took a long drag. "Most folks turn to the police. Wasn't no one for us to turn to. Single woman with a child—my mother was a victim waiting to happen. After every incident, more folks fled. Some with just the clothes on their backs."

They crossed the street to the shuttered club. A padlock hung on the door. A notice from the health department was posted next to it.

"Dropped out of school after the eighth grade," he continued. "That was further than my mother had gone. And she didn't see much use for education. Got my first job here. Mookie and I—he was my friend—we'd hang out at the back door. The workers would call you in to take out the garbage. Sometimes, we'd unload trucks. Made twenty bucks some nights. Wasn't bad for a teenager."

"How long did you do that?"

"'Til I got my license," he said. "Then I started parking cars. Year or two after that, had my little problem with the law."

"What did you do?"

"After I'd park the cars, I'd run the keys over to another building where a copy would be made. And I'd write down the driver's address from the registration in the glove compartment. Day or two later, I'd follow the owner from his home to his job. After he went in and the coast was clear, I'd drive off in the car and take it to a chop shop in Mt. Pleasant. Five hundred a car."

"How'd you get caught?"

"Got greedy," he recalled. "Police caught on somehow. Followed a guy to a garage downtown one day. No sooner than I got in that car and started it, police were all around me, their guns pointed at my face."

"How old were you?"

"Had just turned eighteen the week before. Got five years in Lucasville."

"Five years? For a first offense?"

"It is what it is," he asserted. "Don't blame anyone but myself. Probably saved my life. Got my GED while I was in. Then got my barber's license. When I got out, I didn't look back."

"What about the girl?" she asked.

"What girl?"

"Sugar."

"Like I said before, she worked here. She ran with the boss—the white dude who owned the joint, Adrian Wilson. We got together a couple of times. Nothing serious. Never said nothin' 'bout no baby. And I never heard from her after I went in."

Chapter 6

Christian looked at the clock on Dean Franklin Meriweather's wall and then at the copy of the local newspaper on his desk that displayed a front-page photo of him, several police officers, and Joey entangled on the airport floor. He looked toward the office door as it slowly opened, but it wasn't Dean Meriweather who emerged. Joey peered into the office, rolled her eyes at him, and then ducked back out into the waiting area.

"There's someone already in the office," she disclosed to the dean's assistant.

"Yes," the assistant replied. "The dean's expecting both of you."

Joey took a deep breath before going back inside the office and sitting down in the empty chair beside Christian. She looked forward without greeting him. He trained his eyes on her momentarily before looking away.

"Joey," he uttered.

"Yes," she answered without looking at him.

"I'm sorry about what happened the other day. At the airport."

She turned toward him. "Sorry for what?" she asked. "For knocking me over like a dog? Or for showing up and yelling disgusting things at a Supreme Court judge? Someone invited to speak at our university, no less."

"For knocking you down," he answered. "There's no need to apologize for exercising free speech. Surely you've learned that in your time here?"

She tilted her head and zeroed in on his eyes. "What I've learned is to show people respect, even if I disagree with them. It's called dignity. Grace. Guess you missed that lesson," she suggested.

He shook his head in disbelief. "You don't get it, do you? You folks never do."

"Why don't you educate me? Folks like me."

"Guy gets to the top using every affirmative-action program he can along the way," Christian started. "Then, as soon as he succeeds, he wants to unhook the ladder so that no one else can follow. Because, of course, he did it all on his own. To hell with the folks who died so he could walk into a courtroom without shackles around his ankles."

"How long are you going to need a ladder?" Joey asked. "Do you want to be viewed forever as someone who has to be held by the hand? Like a child? Do you think that really helps us?"

"Guess we'll have to agree to disagree."

"Guess so."

"I'm glad you're okay though," he said. "It wasn't my intention to hurt you. Please believe that. And accept my apology."

"Apology accepted," she said, forcing a smile. "And I'm glad you didn't get arrested. Just what we need—another black man with a record, because we don't have enough of them."

Dean Meriweather walked into the office, reached into the top drawer of his desk, and retrieved two manila folders.

"Morning," he said, handing both Joey and Christian a folder.

"Morning," Joey replied.

"What's this?" Christian asked.

"It's your senior community projects," Meriweather said. "I say 'senior' because you both conveniently put off this requirement until your senior year. You do realize that a community project is a degree requirement at Frederick Douglass University?"

"This isn't about the airport incident?" Joey asked.

"Have I mentioned an airport?" Meriweather asked. "There's a need for two student supervisors at the afternoon recreation program in Lorain. Can't think of two better candidates. All the info you need is in the folders."

"Dean, I really don't like working with children," Joey protested. "There has to be something else."

"You do want to graduate, don't you?" he asked. "And I won't sign off on this requirement, seeing that I have suitable opportunities for both of you. Unless you have something else."

Chapter 7

The employees of the car wash on the north side of the avenue prepared for the day's customers. One folded white towels near the car wash's exit, another carted out a sign announcing the day's specials. As Tobias approached the barbershop, he spotted a police officer a few doors beyond his barbershop writing a ticket. He ran into the shop and grabbed a large broom and dustpan.

"Morning, Toby."

Toby ignored the greeting from Cameron, his longtime colleague, rushed outside, and began sweeping the sidewalk in front of the shop. He'd swept half of it by the time the officer approached.

"Good morning," the officer said, as Tobias swept.

"Morning, Officer," Tobias replied.

"You could sweep your frontage on Mondays before

you close your shop so you won't be in a rush on Tuesday morning," the officer advised him.

"We're closed on Mondays," Tobias said. "Have a nice day, sir."

"You, too."

Tobias was putting the broom and dustpan away when Marcel, the newly hired, young barber, emerged from the back of the shop, carrying supplies to his workstation.

"Morning, Mr. Winslow," he said.

Tobias stood at the closet and glared angrily at him.

"What day is it?" he asked.

"Tuesday, Mr. Winslow," Marcel answered. "Says so right on the calendar."

"Is there somethin' you 'posed to do on Tuesday mornings?"

Marcel stared blankly at Tobias and then adjusted the cloth covering around part of his dreadlocks. "I'm not recalling anything in particular, Mr. Winslow."

Cameron smiled as he applied shaving cream to a customer's face and then instinctively stroked his graying beard.

Tobias sighed deeply as he tried to choose his words carefully. "On Tuesdays—as I've told you the past two weeks—the sidewalk in front of the shop has to be swept before eight a.m. or I'll get a ticket," Tobias scolded.

Marcel smiled. "Good thing you swept it." He laughed. "No fun getting a ticket."

Cameron looked curiously at Tobias and then faced Marcel. "Marcel, it's your job to sweep the sidewalk on

Tuesday mornings," he remarked. "I told you earlier when you got here. It's not for us older men to do."

"You told me that?" Marcel asked.

Tobias chimed back in. "Young man, I'm not gonna tell you again. If I get another ticket, I'm gonna have to add it to your rental fee."

"That don't seem fair," Marcel protested. "It's your shop."

Chante, the stylist who owned the salon connected to the barbershop, entered through the door separating the two businesses. Her short jacket barely covered her skirt and matched her red hat. She adjusted the thermostat on the wall.

"Tobias, we've had this conversation before," she reminded him. "How many times do I have to tell you? You need to make a task list and post it by Marcel's station. And turn this thermostat down. It's too hot in here!"

"Morning, Chante," Tobias said.

She hung her jacket and hat on the coat rack. "Would you like me to print out a list?" she asked. "And could you please, please hang your coat in the back so mine doesn't smell like cigarette smoke?"

Tobias waved a waiting customer into his chair.

Chante walked over to him and whispered in his ear. "I told you when you hired Marcel that he's a little slow," she said. "You have to make things simple for him."

"Whatever," Tobias muttered, shaking his head. "Why do I need to say the same things over and over?"

Cameron placed a warm towel around his customer's chin. "Don't pay no attention to him, Marcel," he commented. "Toby must've got up on the wrong side of the bed today."

"Why such a bad mood today, Tobias?" Chante asked.

"There may be a new woman in my life soon," he said.

Chapter 8

Looking west from the back landing area of the Manor Ridge Nursing Home on the border of Cleveland and Euclid, a trailer park and the roof of a custard stand blocked the view of Lake Erie. To the east of the nursing home, high-rises along Lakeshore Boulevard stood between the facility and the water.

The large fence around sections of the facility prevented viewing the city to the southwest, but there wasn't anything to see in that direction other than a dilapidated shopping center and the ever-expanding blight the two cities shared.

Tobias was well aware of the geography surrounding this place, but it seemed both strange and new on a Sunday. He couldn't recall having ever been here on a Sunday.

As Sundays and Mondays were the two days the barbershop was closed, Tobias's schedule for those days was extremely well-organized. Rest and relaxation on Sundays, with an occasional visit to church. Grocery shopping on Monday mornings as there were usually less shoppers than on Sundays. House cleaning, dry cleaner pickups of his work aprons, and a visit with his elderly Aunt Bessie every other Monday.

As strange as being at the nursing home on a Sunday was the package and subsequent telephone call he'd received from a woman in Elyria informing him of an event at Luke Easter Park, and asking him to escort his aunt to the event. Apparently, his aunt had been one of charter members of Cleveland Chapter of Wilfred Foster Society—at least that's what the woman on the telephone told him—and the leaders wanted to recognize her as one of their oldest living members before it was too late. The package delivered to his home contained a special badge with a gold star on it. As his aunt's closest living relative, altering his schedule this one day to take her to the event was the least hc could do. Though he didn't understand why people would waste time talking about some young man who'd been killed more than fifty years ago, or how his aunt would have ever had time to be part of something like this. Neither she nor his mother had two nickels to rub together. As such, they always seemed engrossed in surviving day-to-day.

Tobias parked the van he'd borrowed from Cameron in the driveway of the facility and patiently waited for the staff to wheel his aunt outside. He smiled as they finally guided her wheelchair down the access ramp toward the minivan. "Hello, Aunt Bessie."

She wore dark sunglasses to protect her eyes. And the nursing-home staff had packed a small bag of things she'd might need during her short trip. The bag rested in her lap.

Under the duffle bag was a light blanket to lay across his aunt to keep her warm.

"Bet you never thought you'd be living on the lake," Tobias said. "Long way from the fields of Louisiana."

She didn't answer.

"Feeling okay, Aunt Bessie?"

"Doing good," she answered in her soft, raspy voice.

Two assistants from the nursing home helped her into the passenger side of the van and then folded her wheelchair and placed it into the back of the vehicle.

"Who you say you was?"

"Tobias, your nephew."

"Tobias?"

"Annabelle's son." He climbed into the driver's seat and shut the door.

"You knew Anna?" she asked. "That was my little sister. Came to Cleveland two, three years 'fore her. Got a job and got settled. She came up after that. Her and her son."

"Yes, Aunt Bessie, I know."

"Worked as a domestic," she continued. "That's what they used to call maids. Anna got on with a white family in Cleveland Heights in one of them mansions along Coventry. Toby, her son, he ain't had much of an education. None of us did. He got hooked up with the wrong crowd, ended up in prison. Say he was running the biggest stolen car ring on the east side. Broke Anna's heart."

As he pulled out of the nursing home's driveway, Tobias pondered whether it would be better to make his way through the city streets to the park, or if he'd be better off getting on the highway. He chose the highway, as the constant movement without stops would likely put his aunt to sleep, and provide a respite from having to hear the same stories over and over.

"My nephew got out of prison and started a business," she said, picking up the story. "But Anna, she died 'fore he got out, and she never seen any of that. Don't think I've seen that boy in a few years. You know Toby?"

He changed the subject. "Looks like a great day for an outdoor get-together," he said. "I'm sure you'll enjoy getting together with friends and talking about Louisiana."

"Louisiana? That's where we come up from. Didn't I tell you that?" She laughed. "Boy, you ain't that bright, are you? Wasn't much there for folks like us," she said, tapping a finger on her hand. "I worked forty years cleaning folks' houses. Sister did too. Left those back woods and ain't never looked back."

"Yes, Bessie," he said. "Should be 'bout twenty minutes or so 'fore we reach the park. The woman who called me said they were planning some interesting events surrounding the young man who was killed."

"Somebody got killed?" she asked. "Damn shame. Can't turn on that television without hearing 'bout this one or that one getting shot. Most of 'em look like you and me. Why they keep killing each other? Their own kind? I try not to pay no attention to it. But they keep that TV on all day."

As he pulled off the highway to go south toward the park, his aunt leaned her head against the window and dosed off. Tobias chuckled to himself as he considered the wisdom of scheduling an event at Luke Easter Park. It would be simpler, he thought, to hang a sign around your neck inviting people to rob you.

Chapter 9

Security guards in bright, yellow T-shirts strategically stood between the event goers and everyone else at the park. Walkie-talkies in hand, they formed a barrier that extended from the parking lot around the amphitheater and alongside the streets intersecting the southeast corner of the park. Within the area cordoned off by the guards, at least twenty-five of them, smoke rose from large, charcoal grilling pits near the parking area, carrying the savory smells of crawfish bisque, gumbo, turtle soup, jambalaya, and other Louisiana favorites past the crowd and onto Kinsman Avenue.

On the amphitheater stage, a dance troupe from Shaw High School in East Cleveland performed while some of those arriving at the event took their places in the seats reserved for the oldest attendees. Tobias positioned Bessie's wheelchair next to the reserved seats and placed the special badge he'd received in the mail on her lap, before walking toward the vending area. He had no interest in hearing about someone who'd presumably been killed before he was even born. He had enough problems of his own. He'd smile, be cordial, and then take Bessie back to the nursing home after a couple of hours. She'd probably sleep through most of event, anyway.

Behind the stage, McKenzie Dubois Frazier glanced at small index cards and rehearsed her address. Her mother, Madeline Dubois, had done a remarkable job of creating the Wilfred Foster Society. There were chapters in five states, monthly inquiries from people seeking information on how to start new chapters, and the group's efforts to compel the US Department of Justice to pursue the case of Foster's decades-old disappearance was attracting national media attention, if not any meaningful government action.

The gatherings of the "Wilfred's Dreamers"—as they had become known—were becoming must-attend events. This was partially attributable to the networking opportunities the events afforded, as doctors, lawyers, accountants, teachers, and business owners were now as numerous as blue-collar workers, even if their genealogic connection to Wilfred Foster was dubious at best. For this reason, most of the events were invitation-only, and people seeking membership into the society had to document a connection to Foster.

McKenzie's husband, Sebastian, prepared the food for the events, and that was also part of the increasing draw. Maddie Dubois had taken the group as far as she could. It was now time for McKenzie to take the reins and move the society in different directions. She planned to use the collective power of the professionals within the society's membership rolls to advance the group's agenda. McKenzie held no hopes that Wilfred Foster's disappearance would ever be solved or that anyone would ever face justice for the crime. She also didn't buy into the legend that Wilfred's mother, Vernita, periodically tormented descendants through visions, and that the visions wouldn't end until someone in Wilfred's family tree was united with someone in his former fiancée's family tree.

No, that was something for the old-timers to hold on to. She preferred to use her time and talents organizing chapters and coordinating their efforts to raise money for college scholarships. She envisioned large fund-raising rallies in Louisiana and in Washington and was hopeful she might even use the group's connections to get former President Barack Obama to address one of their gatherings. And she was finally at a point in her life where she could move full steam ahead with her plans. She and Sebastian and their two children had recently moved into a new home they'd built west of Cleveland in Lorain County, and they had secured a location to open a second restaurant.

Their first restaurant, Sebastian's Place, on the eastside of Cleveland had become a gathering spot for young professionals, and they planned to eventually franchise the concept. If they could only sell the house that they'd recently moved out of. It had sat on the market for nearly two years.

Tobias returned from the vending area and sat in an

empty chair next to Bessie. The crowd applauded the dancers as McKenzie made her way to a microphone. She held an oval sticker in the air. As she did, volunteers began distributing materials to those seated.

"I hope you're enjoying the entertainment and the wonderful food," she started, glancing at her mother in the reserved seats. "But we don't get together simply to eat and to be entertained. You probably can't read this sticker I'm holding. It says, 'I'm a dreamer.' It's included in the material that is being passed out right now."

She smiled as she looked across the crowd. The 300 or so people who'd turned out was a really good showing.

"I'm not going to speak long before I let you get back to the food and the entertainment," she continued. "But there are two things I want to stress. First, the stickers. Please do not leave today without taking at least one. Take as many as you need. I'd like you to place them on your car, display them at your business, in your window at home. And as you travel around, and you see these stickers, if you can, stop and introduce yourselves to your fellow Dreamer. You see, individually, we may not accomplish much. But together, there's no telling what we'll accomplish. And believe me, they don't call us Dreamers for nothing.

"Also in your packet is information about the bimonthly meetings we hold. We try to move the locations around so that at least one is close to everyone. It's at these meeting that you'll learn about specific plans. So, take a sticker. Take two. Display your sticker and commit yourself to meeting your extended family—both through personal interactions throughout the year and by attending a meeting."

Chapter 10

Joey's roommate Rasheeda displayed a slightly puzzled look as she watched her friend from her desk on the other side of their dormitory room. With one hand holding a dress to the light from the window, Joey smiled as she admired the garment's yellow and green pattern, especially how the colors merged. Then, her smile left as quickly as it had arrived, and she tossed the dress onto the pile of other clothes on her bed.

"Really?" Rasheeda said.

"Huh?" Joey replied.

"Is it really that difficult to pick out something to wear?"

Joey didn't immediately answer. She contemplated the question for a moment, and then walked to her closet. "It's my first day," she retorted. "I want to make a good impression. Since you have all the answers, what would you suggest?"

Rasheeda titled her head upward as she glanced into the small mirror she held. Then she gently closed her lips together to smooth out her lipstick. "Jeans. A sweater," she offered. "You did say that the job is at a recreation center working with children."

"You're right," Joey responded. "They'll probably be running around in a gym or outside."

"That *is* what they do at recreation centers," Rasheeda said, smiling. "Are the clothes really what you're stressing about?"

Joey walked over to her bed and sat on it. "Is it that obvious?" she asked.

Rasheeda grinned. "It's that student you have to work with. The one from the airport. You like him, don't you?"

"Wrong," Joey answered. "I'm not studying him."

"You must admit, he's fine."

"Whatever. This may come as a surprise to you, but I really don't like working with children. This is not the volunteer experience I would have chosen."

"C'mon. How bad can it be?"

Joey picked up the outfits on her bed and walked to her closet. "If I wanted to work with children, I'd be studying to be a teacher, not a lawyer," she explained. "Last thing I want to do in my spare time is deal with some misbehaving children. This has got headache written all over it."

"May do you some good."

"How's that?"

"Teach you a lesson or two that you can use when you have your own."

"My own what?"

"Children."

"Please," Joey said. "I don't want any children."

"Your husband might?"

"I'm not thinking about any husband," Joey informed her. "I'm thinking about getting my degree and getting into law school and then a good placement. And being able to repay my student loans before I die."

"You may not be thinking about one *now*, but one day you will," Rasheeda speculated. "Trust me. And you'll regret not taking more time to scope out all the fine candidates here. Black men at a university trying to better themselves. Where are you going to find a better gene pool?"

Joey glared at Rasheeda. "You should spend less time working on your MRS degree and a little more on the other one," she said.

"And you should stop and smell the roses."

Chapter 11

*S*even wooden chairs sat against an exterior brick wall under a large, extended cloth awning facing an open field in the distance. Women dressed in multi-colored gowns sat in each chair, a few methodically rocking back and forth—at least as far as the wood restraining bars across their laps allowed.

In the middle of the row of women, a middle-aged black lady shivered in the late morning breeze. She looked past the open field toward the road with a sense of anticipation as though it held the answers she sought.

Between her and the road in the distance, several unrestrained women walked without purpose in the open field. One moved her hands as if she were turning a steering wheel; another plucked dandelions then blew the seeds upward.

"Ain't nobody seen Wilfred," the black woman said to no one in particular. "Some say them white boys got *hold of him. Took him down to the river." She shook her head no. "I believe he went up north," she proclaimed. "To prepare a place for us. Should be coming back down that road pretty soon. You'll see." She arched her head toward the road. "Willie!" she screamed. "Willie!"*

A woman dressed in a white uniform and hat rushed down the row of wooden chairs until she reached the black woman. "Settle down, Vernita," she demanded, placing her hands on the woman's shoulders. "Settle down. Don't go disturbing the rest of the residents. You settle down now."

෴

"Mr. Winslow. Mr. Winslow! Everything okay?"

Tobias shook his head and instantly felt his consciousness increase as his eyes opened and the doctor standing in front of the door in the exam room slowly came into focus. He lifted his clenched fist to his chest, as if to pound out the mucus, and coughed several times.

"I'm good," Tobias replied. "I'm good. Must've dozed off."

The health clinic on Miles Avenue was probably not the first choice of most of its clients. More likely, it was their only choice since the facility treated people who didn't have medical insurance. The waiting rooms were too small, the television on the wall in the reception area played the same health promotional continually and, because most of its patients were walk-ins, there was a steady stream of young mothers with sick—and fussy—

and often contagious babies. It also attracted folks who, from time to time, felt more comfortable discussing a sensitive matter with a stranger than with the physician who'd been treating them and their family members for years.

Tobias had medical insurance. But he rarely visited the doctor, and it seemed easier to drop by the clinic on those few occasions when he did. He'd have to wait until they got around to him, but as this was a Monday and his shop was closed, he had plenty of time to wait.

After a nurse took his vitals, Tobias was ushered into an exam room, and he waited for what seemed like an hour. He heard muted voices coming from adjoining rooms and could hear people coming and going. He tried to stay alert, but he was tired as he hadn't slept very well since he'd met Donna. Could that boy be his? None of this made any sense.

But the young man in the photo bore a striking re- semblance to his relatives—a bit taller, but with those same slim features and chiseled face. He closed his eyes and prayed that this test would make it all go away, as quickly as it had arrived with that certified letter and the subsequent, long-distance telephone conversation with Donna.

The doctor moved to the exam table and gently placed his fingers against Tobias's throat and neck area. "Really don't like the sound of that cough," he said. "Do you have any pain or tenderness?"

"A little," Tobias answered.

"How long have you had this cough?"

"Two, three weeks."

"I'm going to give you something for it," the doctor announced. "Take it three times a day. If the cough persists for more than three days, I want to see you back here. Okay?"

"Sure."

The doctor walked over to a desk in the exam room and logged onto the computer. "There's also the matter of your blood pressure, Mr. Winslow. Way too high. I'm going to prescribe something for that. You'll take it once a day."

"Okay."

The doctor looked down at Tobias's chart. "A nurse will come in and swab your mouth," he informed Tobias. "The DNA sample will be sent to the lab, as per the instructions you've provided. You'll be able to call that number on the form to get the results. Usually takes a couple of weeks."

"Okay."

"The nurse will also take a blood sample, and then we'll have you on your way."

"What for?"

"Been a while since we've seen you, Mr. Winslow," the doctor commented. "I'd like to check your cholesterol levels and some other things. Do you have any questions for me?"

"No."

"Okay then. I'll either be seeing you in a couple of days, if that cough persists, or in two weeks or so, after

I've had a chance to review the results of your blood work. Understand?"

"Yes."

Chapter 12

A group of college students were seated in a small auditorium at the Horizon Academic Center in Lorain, a former elementary school that now housed a recreation center, a daycare, and several unrelated businesses. On the walls inside the auditorium were pictures of famous African Americans—President Barack Obama, Martin Luther King, Jr., Thurgood Marshall, Rosa Parks, Sojourner Truth, and Muhammad Ali.

Tracy Scott, the director of the recreation center, stood in front of a blackboard. The student volunteers, including Joey and Christian, sat in chairs facing her.

"It's a pretty simple operation," Scott explained. "The students start arriving around four. Their first stop is the cafeteria where they'll get a snack from the counter, find a seat at a table, and eat."

A hand went up. "What kind of snack?"

"Good question," Scott acknowledged. "The snacks are provided by a local nonprofit. Usually it's some sort of sandwich, a piece of fruit, chips, or popcorn. We provide bottled water, but some of the students will buy drinks from the vending machine. Usually, there are two kinds of sandwiches to choose from." She pointed over the heads of the volunteers toward classrooms on the other side of the area in which they sat. "After they eat, the girls will come into one of the classrooms. There are three classrooms," she informed them. "Each student is assigned to a particular classroom, and they will begin working on their homework. The boys go to the gym for activities."

"Do the boys always have gym before the girls?" someone asked.

"Yes," Scott answered. "We find that the boys tend not to be able to concentrate on their work if the work comes before the activity. So we do what seems to work."

Another hand went up. "And the boys and the girls always do the gym part separately?"

"Yes," Scott answered. "We have fewer problems when the boys and girls are separated."

"Problems?"

"Fights," Scott divulged. "Arguments—the things children do."

"And what do we do when there's a fight?"

"Break it up," Scott instructed. "Bring the combatants to my office, and I'll handle it from there. So, when you come in, you'll see your name on a list. That list will tell you where you will go after the snack. You may be in a classroom, or you might be in the gym or outside on the playground."

"How long do they stay in the classroom?"

"Forty-five minutes," Scott answered. "Then they switch. The boys go to the classrooms and the girls go to activity. If you're assigned to a classroom, your job is to make sure they're doing their homework. Each of them has a sheet with assignments, so if they say they don't have any homework, check their sheet and ask them to show you their completed work. And, yes, you can help them with their work. But don't do it for them."

Scott smiled as she looked across the classroom full of volunteers. "I'm so happy all of you are here. It's so important that our young students see people like you. After the second forty-five-minute session, all the students return to the cafeteria. Usually, we'll have some sort of quick lesson. Sometimes a guest speaker. I usually handle the lesson, but don't be surprised if I call on one or two of you to add something to what I'm explaining. Just use personal examples if you have them."

She held up a sheet of paper. "This sheet of paper, which is kept right by the assignment sheet, will list the subjects I'll be speaking on, so it's probably a good idea to take a look at it so you'll be prepared if I call on you. After the lesson, the students will grab a bagged snack that they'll take home with them. Any other questions?"

Chapter 13

Tobias worked on his last customer, Cameron swept up the hair clippings around his workstation, and Marcel organized boxes in the large stockroom connected to the main area of the barbershop.

Chante emerged from the beauty shop, walked over to Cameron, and turned her back to him. Her olive-colored dress had a V-neck and ruffles along the neck and hemline. "Can you get this?"

"Sure thing," Cameron responded. He fastened the small hook at the top of the back of her dress. "Hot date?"

Chante peered into the mirror behind Cameron's workstation and checked her makeup and hair. "Business," she offered. "Ever hear of Antonio Cochran?"

"The businessman?" Cameron asked.

"Yes," she said, turning away from the mirror toward Cameron. "He might be interested in bankrolling an expansion of my business. Can you imagine Chante's Places all over Cleveland—"

"Is that what he's interested in?" Tobias asked, checking out Chante's tight-fighting dress as he did. He began coughing uncontrollably as soon as he finished his question.

Chante shook her head slowly. "See? That's what you get when you hate," she quipped. "Can't a man recognize a good business opportunity when he sees one? Why does it always have to be about *that*?"

"I'm sure he recognized something," Tobias managed in-between coughs.

A young man walked into the shop as Marcel emerged from the stock area.

"Dee," Marcel said. "Dee—"

Deante Walker leaned into Marcel and embraced him. "My nigga," he said in greeting. "'Sup?"

"Surviving," Marcel answered. "Merely surviving."

Deante pulled a small black book out of his pocket.

"Four, five, one, two," Marcel said.

He handed D-man twenty dollars. D-man scribbled the numbers in his book.

Chante walked over and handed him thirty dollars. "Same as usual," she said.

Cameron rifled through his pockets and retrieved twenty dollars. "Same as last week," he said, handing the money to D-man.

Deante approached Tobias. "How 'bout you, Mr. Winslow?" he asked. "Want to try your luck?"

Tobias glared at him without answering.

"D-man," Chante interrupted. "How long have you been coming in here asking him to play?"

Deante smiled.

"Has he ever played?" she asked.

"No harm in asking," D-man noted.

It was not that Tobias had a problem with illegal gambling. In fact, he couldn't understand why the state could operate its casinos and lotteries but regular folks couldn't wager amongst themselves as they had for decades. And he didn't buy the argument that by funneling gambling proceeds through the state some of the money would be used to improve public schools. He'd been in and around enough schools in Cleveland to understand they were getting worse, not better, and that funneling more money into them was a sucker's bet.

No, his problem was D-man. Deante was the splitting image of who Tobias had once been, and he reminded Tobias of his own troubled past every time he visited. Tobias also fully understood that the crowd D-Man ran with spelled trouble with a capital "T," and he didn't want that group to think they were welcome in the barbershop.

Before Tobias's mother died, at a time when they lived in a rented home in Collinwood, she would insist that he drop moth balls into the holes rabbits burrowed around their house and then fill in those holes with dirt several days later, after the irritating scent of the moth balls had repelled the rabbits. Once he asked his mother why she was so obsessed with harmless rabbits.

"It's not the rabbits that concern me," she explained. "It's the things that come after the rabbits."

D-man was no rabbit. But he was bound to attract predators.

A car pulled up outside the shop and the driver blew his horn. Tobias set his clippers aside and looked out the shop's window.

"Chante," he yelled. "Your chariot awaits."

She walked back into the beauty shop and retrieved her coat and purse. As she walked to the front door, she paused by Marcel. "Did you ask him yet?"

"Not yet," Marcel answered.

"Well, what are you waiting for?" she asked, looking at Tobias as she left.

Cameron smiled. "Toby," he said. "I think Marcel has something he wants to discuss with you."

Tobias used a small brush to sweep away hair from his customer's shirt collar. He bid the customer goodbye, and then turned to Marcel. "What is it?"

D-man put away his book and headed to the door. "Catch you later," he said.

"Something you want to ask me, Marcel?" Tobias asked.

"Actually, there is, Mr. Winslow," Marcel started. "Been thinking 'bout the stockroom."

"The stockroom? What about it?"

"Ever think about using it for something else?"

"Like what?"

"What if we turned it into a community gathering spot—where we could host poetry slams, have a weekly reading club?"

Tobias laughed. "Why would I want to do that?" he questioned.

"Might bring in some new customers," Marcel answered. "Would be a way of giving back to the community."

"You think I need a bunch of people hanging out here?" Tobias asked, staring at D-man outside. "Bringing all kinds of trouble to my door?"

"Doesn't have to be that way," Marcel reasoned.

Cameron smiled. "Might be something to what he's saying."

Tobias looked at Cameron. "You think that's a good idea?"

"Just saying," Cameron replied. "Not like we're getting much use out of that space anymore. Other than a spot for you to smoke."

Tobias stood silently with his folded hands covering his mouth. He walked over to his workstation, retrieved the packet of information he'd received at the Dreamer event but had yet to toss in the trash, and removed one of the oval stickers. He placed the sticker in the corner of the shop's front window.

"What's that?" Marcel asked.

"A way to bring in more business," Tobias answered.

Chapter 14

Director Scott walked in front of the podium in the auditorium at the recreation center and then pulled a chair aside and sat facing the students, volunteers, and workers. She smiled at a few of the students as she finished her short talk, glared menacingly at others as a warning to stop whatever else they were doing and to pay attention or risk being publicly embarrassed.

"Courage is not something that we all have," she concluded. "But courage is something we should all seek. And there's a lot of ways to show courage. Doing your best in school while others are loafing, that's courage. Helping out a friend who is being bullied, that's courage. Understand?" She glanced across the auditorium. "Christian, please come up and share a word or two about courage."

Christian diverted his eyes from his phone when he heard his name and looked to the podium. "Huh?" he asked.

"Courage," Scott repeated. "Please come and share a thought with us about courage."

"Sure," he said, slowly rising. He tucked the phone away and walked to the podium. Once up front, he scanned the room, picking spots beyond the students and volunteers on which to focus, as he'd been taught in his public speaking class. Not too high—about eye level—so no one could tell he was looking past them. "Courage," he started. "As Mrs. Scott said, it's not something that everyone possesses. But even if you don't have it today that doesn't mean you can't have it tomorrow. Take Joseph. Now he had courage."

He walked in front of the podium. "Joseph had the courage to say no to Potiphar's wife when she wanted him to sleep with her. He recognized that was wrong. And he had the courage to say 'I will not do this despicable thing.' It's not always easy to do what's right. Sometimes, it's a lot easier to go along with the crowd. But it's takes courage to be different. Any questions?"

Several hands went up.

"Who's this Joseph?" one girl asked.

"He was Jacob's son," Christian answered. "In the Bible."

"So why didn't he sleep with Potiphar's wife?" one boy asked. "Was she ugly? Did she have AIDS? And what kind of stupid name is Potiphar?"

The students started laughing. Before Christian could answer, Scott interrupted.

"Our time is up," she said. "Make sure you pick up your snack on the way out."

As the students filed out, Scott grasped Christian's hand. "I think you've just learned a good lesson," she said.

"What would that be?" he asked.

"You have to reach these children where they are. Now me, I really appreciate you retelling that story about Joseph. It tells me a lot about you. I'm guessing you went to church every Sunday?"

"Yes."

"Me too," she said. "But most of these students are not acquainted with church or the Bible, let alone Joseph. Now, quote one of these rappers or reality TV stars and they're right with you."

"Don't you think that's sad?"

"It is. Still, we must find ways to reach them. Our future depends on it."

❧❧❧

"So how are you feeling this morning?"

Tobias struggled to smile in response to the doctor's question. His smile wasn't very convincing, much more polite than authentic. But he managed to offer, "Taking it day by day. That's all I can do."

"That's all any of us can do," the doctor responded.

The doctor logged onto the computer on the portable work station and retrieved Tobias's records. He studied them for a moment before turning to Tobias. "Mr. Winslow," he started. "Your cholesterol levels are high. I'm going to prescribe something for that. You'll take it once a day. Are you allergic to anything?"

"Not that I'm aware of."

"Okay. We'll try atorvastatin, twenty milligrams. It's on the generics list at most pharmacies, so it won't cost much. But it's important that you take it daily."

"I can do that."

The doctor picked up the telephone on the wall and waited for the person on the other end to answer. "Hello, Dr. Vincent here. Do we have any more of those blood pressure kits? Okay, good. Can you bring one to Room Sixteen? Thanks."

A few moments later, a nurse entered the room and handed a small box to the doctor. He opened it, and then handed the box to Tobias.

"This is a blood pressure monitor," he said. "I'll have the nurse show you how to use it. I want you to take your blood pressure in the morning when you get up, and at night before bed."

Tobias nodded in agreement.

Dr. Vincent held up a small book that was in the box. "Log the numbers each time and bring the book back with you for your next visit. Have you tried to quit smoking?"

Tobias looked down at this shirt pocket to see if his pack of cigarettes was visible. They weren't, but his clothes reeked of smoke. A dead giveaway. "Once or twice," he answered. "Never had much luck."

"Well, we have several programs that some people have found useful," Dr. Vincent said, handing Tobias a brochure. "You can read about them and call the number if you're interested. It's never too late to quit."

"Thanks."

"Well, okay then. The nurse will show you how to use this monitor at home." Dr. Vincent extended his hand. "Good luck, Mr. Winslow."

"Thank you, Doctor."

Chapter 15

A loud buzzer rang. A guard slid a heavy metal door open and escorted Tobias into a large room. Throughout the room, men dressed in orange jumpsuits sat at small metal tables bolted to the floor, across from people dressed in regular clothes. Some were smiling, others cried, a few joked and teased as if they were home in their living rooms.

Tobias scanned the room for Avery Higgins and then began walking to a frail-looking man seated at one of the tables.

The man used the table to lift himself as Tobias approached. "Look what the cat done drug in," Higgins mused.

Tobias embraced him. "How you been, Mookie?"

"Surviving, Toby. Surviving."

Tobias sat across from Mookie. He glanced across the room at the sea of mostly black and brown faces and then at the guards stationed throughout. Women, children, mothers, fathers, and siblings—all trying to share private moments in public. "You ever gonna get outta this place?" Tobias asked.

"Gave up that hope a long time ago," Mookie admitted. "I'll die in here one way or another—either by heart attack or shank. What brings you to my humble abode?"

"Trying to get some things straight in my head," Tobias confessed. "This is as good a place to start as any."

"Well," Mookie declared, "my time is yours. Might not be enough time to get things straight in that head of yours, though."

Tobias smiled. As he did, a guard moved quickly past him to the other side of the room.

"Apart over there!" the guard shouted. "Sit down!"

The guard pointed his billy club at a couple getting a bit too frisky.

"Toby," Mookie chimed in, regaining his friend's attention. "What were you saying?"

"Oh, yeah," Tobias continued. "Been thinking 'bout my case. How it all went down. Why Mr. Wilson sent me on that job alone that day, being that he had never done that before."

Mookie smiled. "You drove all the way down here from Cleveland to ask me that? 'Bout something that happened decades ago?"

"Just wondering," Tobias answered. "That's always struck me out as odd."

Mookie stared intently into Tobias' eyes. "You wouldn't be accusing me of something?"

Tobias looked over at one of the guards, then back at Mookie. "No, no," he assured Mookie.

Even if Mookie had somehow been involved, which Tobias doubted, he had long since walked away from that life. And if he allowed something to suck him back into it, especially something like accusing his old friend of either setting him up or knowing about it and remaining silent, he'd soon be sitting next to Mookie in orange garb.

"Then what? You think Wilson set you up?"

"That's the only thing that's making any sense."

"Even if he did, what difference does that make after all these years? You moved on ages ago. Wish I had."

"Might not be that simple."

"Why not?"

"Remember Sugar, Wilson's girlfriend? Worked at Malcolm's."

Mookie smiled. "Man, she was hot," he recalled. "Nice long legs and that gorgeous smile. You were sweet on her."

"Do you recall what happened to her after I went in?"

"Can't say that I do. Wasn't long after that that I caught my own case," Mookie pointed out. "Don't believe I saw her after that. Ain't thought about that sweet thing since."

"I think she might've been pregnant," Tobias said.

"Sugar? What that got to do with you?"

"Might've been mine. I may have had a son."

"Had?"

"He's dead."

Mookie paused. "So, you think Wilson found out 'bout you and Sugar, then set you up."

"It's possible," Tobias conceded. "Probably likely."

"What's Sugar got to say 'bout all this?"

"She's dead too," Tobias observed. "I'm thinking she either left when she was pregnant or after she had her baby. To get away from Wilson. Or he paid her to leave—to disappear."

"That's sounds like that weasel. He wouldn't have taken kindly to such a betrayal," Mookie said. "Why you telling me this? If Sugar's dead and the son's dead, what's the issue?"

"The son had a daughter," Tobias added.

Mookie looked around to make sure nobody else was eavesdropping. He then leaned closer to Tobias. "If a man did that to another man, he should pay," Mookie whispered. "It's only right that he pays. Did you really need to drive all this way for me to tell you that?"

Tobias looked across the room at the other prisoners. "Do you remember why our families came north years ago?" he asked.

"To get away from all the stuff that was happening down South," Mookie answered.

"Ever think that we became worse than the people we were running from?" Tobias asked.

Mookie used the table to lift himself up. "A rat can't become more of a rat than his mother."

Chapter 16

In one of the classrooms at the recreation center, several volunteers worked individually with students. One volunteer diagrammed a math problem; another quizzed a student on history, while Joey tried to help a small child sound out a word.

"Okay," Joey said calmly. "Let's try it again."

She took a small piece of construction paper and covered part of the word on the paper in front of Tonya, who sat across from her at a small table.

"You can do this," Joey encouraged her. She smiled, pointing down at the paper. "Take it slow."

She slid the construction paper to reveal the first part of the word.

"Col...Col...Col—um," Tonya pronounced. "Col-um."

"That's good," Joey complimented. "Colum."

She covered the first part of the word with the construction paper and revealed the last part of it.

Tonya looked down at the last part of the word and smiled.

"Bus," she blurted out confidently. "Bus."

"That's right," Joey confirmed. "Very good. Now all together."

She removed the construction paper.

"Colum—bus," Tonya said. "Columbus. Like the city."

Joey grasped her hand. "Yes!" she said. "Columbus. See? You can do this. Now, put your work away, and we'll join your friends in the gym."

Tonya put her papers and books into her backpack then followed Joey down the hallway to the gym. As they neared the gym, a young boy raced past, knocking Joey and Tonya to the side.

"Davon!" Joey shouted. "Hold it right there! Haven't we told you not to run in the hallway?"

"Yes, Miss Joey," he answered, looking away from her, embarrassed.

"And pull up your pants—you think I want to see your underwear?"

He put his head down.

"Do you need me to buy you a belt?"

Tonya giggled.

"No, ma'am," he said, lifting his head. "Can I go now?"

"Do you think that you should apologize?"

"Sorry, Miss Joey," he apologized.

Davon and Tonya disappeared. Joey hovered outside Director Scott's office until she was waved inside.

"Everything okay, Joey?" Scott asked.

Joey forced a smile as she sat in one of the chairs between Scott's desk and the door. "Help me to understand this," she stated. "Every day, we tell Davon and at least twenty other boys to pull up their pants. Over and over again. Why do we do that?"

Scott looked up from her desk. "Because walking around with your pants hanging off your butt is disrespectful," she answered. "Unacceptable."

"Yes, I understand that," Joey agreed. "I mean, why do we keep giving them chance after chance, with little or no consequences?"

"What do you suggest we do?"

"I'm not exactly sure, but there ought to be some sort of consequence for disobedience. If there's not, then what are we really teaching them?"

"Tell me again what your major is?" Scott asked.

"Pre-law."

"Well, one of the reasons you're here—and believe me, I do appreciate all of you volunteers—but you're here because these children need to meet people who are, or who are going to be, doctors, lawyers, dentists. They need to believe that they can set goals and achieve them."

"With all due respect, what does that have to do with these boys running around with their pants hanging off their butts?" Joey inquired. "Do you think the person doing the hiring at the supermarket or at the fast-food restaurant is going to ask them to pull up their pants? Or move on to the next person? The person who dresses appropriately?"

"The person's going to move on," Scott noted. "But they're not at the supermarket. Not yet. They're at the after-school recreation program. And if we don't tell them and show them how they should act and dress, who will?"

"Their parents?" Joey suggested.

"Wish it were that simple," Scott fretted. "Right now, when you see many of these kids, you see problems. Believe me, I see problems too. But I also see possibilities. There's a possibility that if I keep telling and showing these children how to carry themselves, one or two of them might catch on. And one day, they might be sitting across the desk from me on their way to becoming a lawyer or a doctor."

Joey stood. "I hope you're right."

ↂↄↂↄ

Sebastian Frazier paused at the traffic light. Instead of turning left and continuing toward his restaurant, he proceeded straight through the intersection and turned into a convenience store. He'd promised his wife Kenzie and his mother-in-law Maddie that'd he'd try to stop and introduce himself whenever he saw the oval Dreamer sticker displayed on a window or bumper sticker.

He'd seen one days earlier, truth be told, but it was on a car that was speeding in a different direction. There was no way he was going to follow some random person, especially a woman, and then approach her on the street. But when he saw one of the stickers displayed on the front window of a barbershop, he felt bad about driving past it. So he turned his car around, drove a half mile back to the business, and then looked for a parking spot close enough to the barbershop that could be seen from inside the business. His backseat and trunk were filled with items from the restaurant supply store, and he feared someone might break into his car if he didn't keep an eye on it.

When he entered the shop, Cameron was working on a customer. Tobias and Marcel sat in their chairs staring up at the television. One of the cable channels was looping through its stories.

"Good morning, sir," Tobias said. "Can I help ya?"

Sebastian smiled as he pointed to the Dreamer sticker displayed in the window. "I was wondering about your sticker," he said. "The one in the window."

Cameron looked over at Tobias.

"Got that at an event at a park a couple of weeks ago," Tobias informed Sebastian. "Was hoping it would attract some new customers."

"At Luke Easter Park?" Sebastian inquired.

"Yeah. Were you there?"

"For sure. I did the food," Sebastian said. "I own the Cajun place on Larchmere, down the block from the pub and the gas station." He extended his hand. "I'm Sebastian Frazier."

Tobias smiled. "Tobias Winslow. That was some excellent grub. Especially that soup. What was it?"

"Thanks," Sebastian replied. "Turtle soup. You a Dreamer?"

"My Aunt Bessie is. She can't drive anymore so I brought her to the park."

Sebastian thought for a second. "Your aunt? By marriage or by blood?"

"My mother's sister," Tobias explained.

"Then that makes you a Dreamer too," Sebastian explained, smiling and holding out his arms. "Guess we're family."

"Guess so."

"If you liked the soup, you ought to stop by my place. I take care of family," Sebastian said. "Can't wait to tell my wife that I ran into another Dreamer today. I'd promised her I'd introduce myself whenever I saw one of the stickers. She'll be so proud of me. Have you seen any of the stickers displayed since the event?"

"No," Tobias said.

Even if he had, Tobias would have never approached some stranger to talk about some connection they may or may not have. The entire Dreamer movement seemed to him a waste of time. Didn't folks have enough problems of their own?

As he glanced across the shop, Sebastian noticed a board filled with notices, business cards, and random photos—mostly posted by Marcel. There was one of a rapper who Marcel said would one day be famous, another of a former Cleveland Browns player, who sat in one of the barber's chairs smiling and displaying the peace sign.

"I'm trying to sell a house. Actually, my wife and I have been trying to unload it for more than a year," Sebastian elaborated. "Would you mind if I posted one of my flyers on your board?"

"Why not?" Tobias asked. "We're family. Where's the house?"

"Beachwood."

Chapter 17

In one corner of the Shaker Heights Library, a mix of teenagers, young adults, and older adults sat in three rows of chairs, fixated on the computer screens in front of them. Tobias wondered what was so fascinating on those computer screens, wondered if he could find something on one of those computers that could keep him out of this sticky predicament with Lakisha.

At the other end of the library, parents and children sat on a multi-colored rug. Some played with toys. Others read books or magazines. Between the two areas, other patrons read books, talked on telephones, or worked at the tables situated throughout the room.

A long line of people waited to check out library materials. Others waited in line in front of the reference desk. Near the library's entrance, a security guard sat behind a small, elevated workstation. Tobias settled down at one of the tables in the middle of the spacious room.

He'd placed a newspaper and several magazines on the table and then sat there for an hour without opening any of the periodicals. Instead, he examined the envelope that he'd received in the mail several days earlier. He closed his eyes and silently prayed, at least as best as he understood how. It had been quite some time since he'd been in a church, so he wasn't quite sure how to pray. He prayed that the young man killed in Los Angeles was not his son, that the little girl left behind was not his grand-daughter. How could he care for a girl?

The line at the reference desk didn't seem to be getting any smaller. Tobias returned the periodicals to the shelves and then headed toward the security guard at the exit. He wanted to open the envelope but feared the results. He considered tossing it into the trash and ignoring any further inquiries from Donna. Tobias stood inches away from the security officer.

"Can I help you, sir?" the security guard asked.

Tobias opened the envelope and handed it to him.

"What's this?" the security officer asked.

"What does the number say?" Tobias asked.

The security guard cast a puzzled look at Tobias before removing the letter from the envelope.

"Ninety-nine-point-four percent," the guard answered.

Chapter 18

As Joey stepped into the break room at the recreation center, Christian sipped coffee and perused the local newspaper, a sandwich and bag of chips in front of him. Joey rolled her eyes and turned to leave.

"No need to do that," he suggested without looking up.

"Excuse me," she responded, not turning toward him.

"This is the break room," he said. "You shouldn't feel uncomfortable coming in here. I was finishing up anyway. I'll leave."

She slowly turned toward him. "You're right," she conceded. "There's really no reason for either of us to leave."

He looked up. "You sure?"

She didn't answer. Instead, she sat down at the other end of the small table and began taking items out of a brown paper bag—a chicken salad sandwich, celery sticks, and bottled water. "For what it's worth," she initiated, "I appreciated you using Joseph as an example of courage. Kind of sad that so many of the students didn't understand the reference."

"Tell me about it." He grimaced. "Can I ask you something?"

"What?"

"What do you think about this place?"

She paused. "The facilities are really nice. They could probably use more workers," she answered. "And certainly there's a big need for this place."

"No," he interjected. "That's not what I meant. The students? Academically? Socially?"

"Depressing," she admitted. "Many of them don't read at their grade level. And they haven't mastered things that they should have learned well before now."

"And then there's the matter of how they behave," he added. "Or misbehave."

"Yeah, I've noticed that, too," she mused, laughing nervously. "It's not like they don't master *some* things. They can tell you the words to any song or what happened last night on any of the television shows."

"Or demonstrate the latest dance."

"Do you realize that these children are our future? The future of the black community?"

"Please," he responded. "I don't want to think about that."

"It's all I can think about when I'm here," she exclaimed. "It's scary. Downright scary."

"You're right. It is," he agreed. "Unless we all find some way to get this train back on the track, this problem is going to overtake all us."

"Already has," she said, pointing at the newspaper.

∾∾

"Hello. I'm Detective Arnold."

The police officer who'd entered the barbershop was a husky man—standing in front of the entrance, he practically blocked all the light attempting to sneak past him into the business. His belly extended past his belt, and his hair was combed from one side of his head to the other to cover a bald spot. An American flag pendant was attached to his suit jacket.

"I'm investigating a shooting that happened earlier today across street, down the block," Arnold stated. "Next to the old hamburger stand." The detective walked through the barbershop, handing out his business cards. The few people in the shop smiled and accepted them. "If anyone heard or saw anything, I'd appreciate your help," he urged. "We can't solve these killings without you." He stopped in front of Tobias. "You hear or see anything, sir?"

"Well, as loud as these young folks keep this music in here, hard to hear anything outside sometimes," Tobias pointed out.

"So you didn't notice anything?"

"No."

The detective walked to the front of the shop and looked out at the crime scene down the street. If anyone had been seated in the waiting area, they would have had a perfect view of the lot. Anyone in the shop probably would have also heard gunshots. He looked at Cameron. "You didn't see anybody running?" he asked. "Didn't hear any commotion?"

"Ain't nobody here seen anything, Officer," Cameron answered. "You wasting your time. My time. And time is money."

The detective stood in the middle of the shop and glanced at everyone there. "Today they're shooting outside," he said. "Tomorrow, they'll be shooting in here. We can't get these punks off the street if no one is willing to help."

"You're here to help?" Tobias asked. "Help us like you helped those folks you pumped hundreds of bullets into after their car backfired? Or that boy with the toy gun?"

"All I'm asking for is a little cooperation," Arnold retorted. "If you think of something that might help, call me." The detective walked to the door and then paused and turned around. "All we hear downtown is that we're not doing enough to keep these neighborhoods safe. But how can you help folks who won't help themselves?"

Tobias looked at the detective. "Sir," he said. "I respect what you're saying, but this is Cleveland."

"What does that mean?" Arnold asked.

"Two things," Tobias said. "Somebody's gonna get shot today. Possibly two or three somebodies. And the job is gonna go to someone who looks like you."

"Huh?"

"Somebody white," Tobias stated.

Chapter 19

So, how's this gonna go?" Tobias asked.

Donna had just met Tobias near the baggage claim area at LAX. He'd already retrieved his bag when she arrived.

"Sorry I'm late," she said. "Traffic was horrible. Why don't we get you to the hotel and settled in? Then we can talk about the next step. I've collected some things for you. Things that might help you relate."

She handed him a small duffle bag.

"Like what?"

"Well," she answered. "There are some photo albums, a couple of DVDs. They might help you piece together some of the history."

"Okay."

"We can also visit your son's gravesite if you'd like."

"Can we just get outta here?" he suggested. "I need a smoke."

As they headed for the airport garage, Tobias felt overdressed in his jacket and tie as folks rushed by him in each direction in shorts and T-shirts. He hadn't been sure how one was supposed to dress for such an occasion. Inside the car, as Donna slowly made her way to the airport exit, Tobias shivered. He closed his eyes and slowly took deep breaths.

"You can roll down that window and smoke if it helps," she offered.

"You sure?" he asked.

"Yes."

"Thanks."

He lit a cigarette and took a long drag.

She stared at him. "The window," she instructed.

"Oh," he responded, pressing the small lever that opened the window. "I'm sorry." He closed his eyes, held the cigarette in front of him, and the shivering slowly began to decrease. "Don't think I can do this," he mumbled.

"We don't have to go by the gravesite."

"No," he replied. "I'm not sure I can be what you want me to be for this girl."

"Your granddaughter."

"Right now, that's just a word," he countered. "Has absolutely no meaning. Calling someone a grandfather don't make them one. Do you really think it's smart to uproot her? After all she's been through?"

"It wouldn't be today or tomorrow," she advised. "We wouldn't do anything until the timing's right, with school and everything. But yes, it's probably best that she be with family. It's the only thing she has left."

He couldn't imagine that he—a small-time business owner with a felony record and absolutely no parenting skills—could be all that was left for Lakisha. Why couldn't they place her with some well-meaning couple in the suburbs? He didn't know much about Los Angeles, but would inner-city Cleveland be any better? And wouldn't someone with parenting skills be preferable to someone who didn't have any, even if they weren't family?

Tobias extinguished the cigarette and then began coughing into his hand.

"You okay?"

"I'll be okay," he said. "But I don't think you understand. I ain't never taken care of anything or anybody but myself. And I don't even do a great job of that as you can see."

She reached over and put her hand over his. "Mr. Winslow, I can't begin to imagine what a shock all of this must be," she acknowledged. "I can tell you that we'll provide every resource you'll need. Social workers. Mental health professionals. Academic counselors. We're already working with social services in Cuyahoga County. We're putting together a team, and they will be with you every step of the way."

He flicked his half-smoked cigarette out the window and then closed it.

"Let's take this one step at a time," she suggested.

"I'm not sure about this," he lamented.

Chapter 20

The driver eased the charter bus into a parking spot along the sidewalk. The music blaring from the rear of the bus stopped, and several of the FDU students began to stand and stretch in the aisle. Professor Khaleed got up from his seat at the front of bus, adjusted his kufi, and then switched on a wireless microphone. He pointed to the building outside and then spoke softly and slowly into the microphone.

"This is the last stop on today's tour," he informed the students. "The Phyllis Wheatley Association. Unfortunately, we're running a bit late, so there's not really time to go in and explore. Instead, we'll relax here for a few moments while we talk about the significance of this place. Then, we'll head back to campus. Anybody know who Phyllis Wheatley was?"

Joey raised her hand. "She was the first black poet."

"Yes, Joey," Prof. Khaleed affirmed. "She didn't start this association, but it was named after her. And this isn't the original location or the original name. When it was established in 1911, it was called the Working Girls' Home Association. It was a place where black girls and women were provided housing and job services. Sound like a good idea?"

No one responded.

"Not everyone was happy about it," the professor continued. "In fact, it was very controversial back then. Many, many members of the black community opposed it. Anybody know why?"

Joey again raised her hand. Professor Khaleed walked over to her seat and put his hand over hers.

"Somebody else," he said softly. "Somebody else."

A young man at the back of the bus stood.

"Yes, Vondell?"

"I'm guessing it was probably seen as a conspiracy to keep the black man down by elevating black sisters," Vondell opined.

His answer prompted laughter throughout the bus. Professor Khaleed stared at him.

"Please sit down," Khaleed commanded. "Anyone else?"

No one else offered an opinion.

"Well, it came to be known as the black YWCA. Many in the black community opposed it—not because they didn't need or want the services it provided, but because they thought the YWCA should be providing them.

Can you guess why the YWCA wasn't?" the professor asked.

Christian raised his hand. "Because they didn't serve black people," he correctly answered. "The 'Christian' in their name didn't include us."

"Exactly," Professor Khaleed said. "So that left blacks with a decision to make. Provide these services themselves or wait until others did. It's the same debate we have today, whether we should be doing for ourselves or waiting for someone else to do things for us."

"It's not that simple," Christian commented. "We pay taxes like everyone else, so we deserve our fair share of services. But at the end of the day, there are times when we have to do for ourselves."

"And what responsibilities are ours?" Professor Khaleed asked.

Joey interrupted, looking directly at Christian as she did. "The government should provide a safety net for the vulnerable," she suggested. "Especially the elderly, the poor, and the young."

Christian smiled as he looked at Joey. "But that does not relieve people from doing what they can for themselves," he said. "To lift themselves up."

"Well said, Joey, Christian," Professor Khaleed praised. "Well said. Again, we don't have time to go inside today. But I do urge you to visit this place on your own. There's a lot of local history here."

Vondell stood.

"Yes?" Professor Khaleed asked.

"If you come, come during the day," Vondell urged.

"Why's that?"

"This is Cleveland," Vondell proclaimed. "The only thing that's certain is that someone will get shot today. And it'll probably happen on the east side."

Chapter 21

Vernita looked past her plate of eggs, grits, and ham. To one side of her, a woman shoveled food into her mouth, not looking away from her plate. At the other end of the table, an aide fed another woman.

"Open up," the aide instructed before placing a spoon with a small amount of applesauce into the woman's mouth. "Good. That's good."

Vernita clenched her fists, gritted her teeth, and began breathing heavily. She abruptly stood and glanced across the cafeteria. Then she knocked the items off her tray unto the floor. "He ain't coming back!" she screamed. "They kilt my son! They kilt Wilfred!"

Several aides rushed over and wrestled her to the ground. One of the aides signaled for a strait jacket.

ℰ◯ℰ◯

Tobias jolted himself awake from his nightmare. He

coughed in between taking several deep breaths. He looked at the alarm clock next to the hotel bed. Seeing it was four a.m., he pushed the small clock away.

"I've got to get some sleep," he mumbled. "Got to rest."

He lay silently momentarily and then maneuvered his body to the edge of the bed. Reluctantly, he accepted the fact that he was wide-awake and turned on the lamp on the nightstand. He opened the curtains and peered at the avenue that ran alongside the hotel. A few cars navigated the road under the still-illuminated street lights. He closed the curtains and sat at the small desk in the room, taking notice of the no-smoking sign near the light switch.

He opened one of the photo albums Donna had given him and randomly selected a page. He examined a photo of a young boy, presumably Elton, standing next to Sugar on a beach. Between Sugar and Elton, next to the water, a teenaged boy stood beside a canoe, holding a fish by its tail. The water in the distance seemed to become a darker blue as it stretched to the horizon. Tobias had never seen the California coast, but the scene in the photo seemed more exotic than Southern California. As the teenager next to the canoe looked Mexican, he figured the photo had been taken in Cancun or perhaps Mexico City.

Tobias smiled as he looked at Sugar's legs, high cheekbones, and professional-looking hairdo. What had she ever seen in him, an uneducated teenager on the fast track to prison? He assumed Sugar's Achilles' heel was her poor choice in men. First, she'd latched onto the philandering Wilson. Then, she'd crossed Wilson with him. Both would deal with the consequences for decades.

He considered the next photo—an elementary school-aged boy standing in front of a large poster board smiling. The title on the poster board was "Damage Caused by Oil Spills." Pictures framed on construction paper were affixed to the poster board. Perhaps Elton had finished high school and had acquired more book smarts than Tobias had.

The next photo was of Elton dressed in a baseball uniform holding a bat. He appeared lean and muscular and projected a sense of confidence as he looked into the camera. Tobias smiled as he reveled in the thought that Elton had excelled in sports. He'd always wondered how he would have done in sports if he had the time for such trivial pursuits. While he was hustling to help his mother make ends meet, other children his age were playing sports, going to proms, and attending graduations. He was convinced he would have been a stud running back if given a chance. Running through holes would have been a lot easier than stealing cars and hanging outside of clubs begging for odd jobs.

In the next photo, Elton was dressed in a cap and gown, embracing his smiling mother. Tobias assumed this was from the boy's high school graduation and was happy to think the boy had gone further in school than he had. Tobias closed the photo album and crawled back into the bed.

Chapter 22

Christian slowly nodded his head up and down to the music as he drove away from the recreation center. He was happy to be done for the week and was looking forward to the end of the semester when this volunteer opportunity would end. About a mile down the road, he steered his car to the center of the road as he passed a disabled vehicle on the shoulder.

He gazed into his rearview mirror after he drove around the disabled vehicle. As he did, he watched Joey emerge from the side of the disabled car. He looked at the clock and then glanced again into the rearview mirror. He pulled onto the shoulder, tires crunching in the dirt.

He tried to erase the memory of Joey's condescending tone in the dean's office, tried to forget the look of disgust on her face when she encountered him in the break room, but couldn't.

Still, his conscience would not allow him to keep

driving. He put his car into reverse, activated his flashers, and then slowly rolled back to her car. He stopped a few feet away and got out.

"You okay?" he asked, emerging from his car.

"I've got a flat," she said, staring into her phone. "And I'm supposed to be somewhere in an hour."

"You call someone?"

"Yes," she answered. "But they're not sure how long it's going to be."

He walked to the passenger side of Joey's car and kneeled down beside the front tire. "Looks like you ran over a nail or something," he advised. "You got a spare?"

"Huh?"

"A spare tire."

She looked puzzled.

"Pop the trunk," he directed. He looked inside the trunk before walking back toward his car. "You've got a temp," he noted.

He opened his trunk and took out his jack and tire iron. He placed them next to her front tire and took off his jacket.

"What are you doing?" she asked.

"Changing your tire," he said. "Unless, of course, you'd rather sit here on the side of the road waiting until it gets dark."

"Really," she said, "you don't have to do that. I mean, I'd understand if you didn't."

"Don't be silly."

He unhinged the temporary tire from the bottom of her trunk and took it to the front of the car.

"That looks too small," she observed. "You sure it's the right size?"

"Like I said, it's a temp. You're only supposed to use it for so many miles. It'll give you time to get another tire or fix this one."

He loosened the tire lugs, positioned the jack under the car frame, and began hoisting the car upward. She stopped him.

"You're going to ruin your pants," she pointed out. She retrieved a blanket from her trunk and placed it beside him. "Put this under your knees."

"Thanks," he replied.

He removed the flat and put on the temporary tire. Then, he carried the flat to the trunk. "I know a garage in town that'll fix this," he said.

"Huh?"

"Plug the hole where the nail is," he said. "This is still a good tire. Plenty of tread. No use getting rid of it."

She looked puzzled.

"I'll tell you what," he offered. "I'll drop it off in the morning to see if it can be fixed."

"Thank you so much," she bubbled, grasping his hand. "You have no idea how much this means to me."

She reached into her pocket and pulled out twenty dollars.

"What's this for?" he asked.

"Your help," she said. "Your time."

"Not necessary," he said. "You keep that. I'll tell you what it costs to plug the tire tomorrow. Keep that for the garage."

"You sure?"

"I'm good," he affirmed. "Don't you have someplace to go?"

Chapter 23

The 1950s-themed diner near Tobias's hotel was surprisingly full, considering the morning rush period had passed and lunchtime hadn't arrived. He wasn't sure if the customers were tourists dragging themselves out of bed late or others simply enjoying brunch. An old, catchy tune was playing on one of the miniature jukeboxes at each table. He remembered the words to the song, but couldn't recall its name or artist.

"So are you ready for this?" Donna asked, interrupting his scattered thoughts.

Tobias sipped his coffee as he considered the question. Then, he finished off his first helping of pancakes. "Can't say that I am," he confessed. "Can't say that I'm not."

"Well," Donna continued. "This is how it's going to go. Tomorrow afternoon, you'll meet Lakisha at the social services agency in a special room we have set up for such meetings. I'll be there with you."

"And what am I supposed to say to her?"

"Introduce yourself. Talk to her. Listen." Donna reached across the table and grasped Tobias's hand. "Be yourself," she urged. "This is new to her too. And she's been through more than any young girl should have to go through."

He lifted his cup slightly and motioned to the waitress for a coffee refill. "What if she asks me about Sugar?"

"Answer honestly."

"You think she can handle the truth? Think she needs to know that?"

"Why don't we cross that bridge when you get there?" Donna suggested.

"What's she been told?" Tobias asked.

"She knows that she has a grandfather who lives in Cleveland, where her grandmother was from. She's been told that you've come to LA to meet her. The conversation hasn't gone past that."

A waitress interrupted them. She retrieved Tobias's empty plate and sat down a new one with more pancakes. He reached for the syrup.

Donna stared at the stack. "You've consumed more carbs in this sitting than I do in two days," she commented.

"You assessing my health now too?" he asked.

"If something happens to you, we're back at square one," she explained. "So, yes, it's important that you take care of yourself. For Lakisha's sake." Donna placed a bill on the table as she rose from her seat. "I'll pick you up at the hotel around four p.m.," she reminded him.

"Okay."

Chapter 24

Tobias slowed the rental car to a stop along the sidewalk. He checked the sign on the post nearest him to make sure he could park there. Then he checked the address on the apartment complex across the street against the one in the newspaper article he'd printed from the computer in the hotel lobby.

"Eight Seventy-Five Cordova," he mumbled to himself.

An open house sign hung on the front wall of the complex. A man in a bright blazer stood near the sign holding a clipboard. Tobias exited the car and crossed the street, walking to the man with the clipboard.

"Good morning, sir," the man said, greeting him. "Here for the open house?"

"Huh?" Tobias asked.

"The open house," the man repeated, pointing to the complex's front entrance. "The model's right through the gate to the left."

"Thanks," Tobias responded.

He walked past the first agent to the gate, glancing at the newspaper article as he did. "Apartment Two-H," he mumbled.

Another agent greeted him inside the model apartment.

"Morning, sir," she said. "If you could please sign the register, we'd appreciate it."

"Morning," Tobias responded.

He scribbled his name on the list, and the agent handed him a business card.

"Feel free to look around," she suggested. "If you have any questions, let me know."

Tobias examined her business card.

"Is apartment Two-H available, Miss Gilford?" he asked.

She looked at her list.

"Not sure if that one's ready yet," she answered. "I can find out for you, though. It's exactly like this one."

"That would be great," he commented. "I'm Mr. Winslow."

"Well, Mr. Winslow," she stated. "This is a two-bedroom, one bath. It's been freshly painted, and there's new carpet throughout. The crown molding was just added."

"Very nice," he noted.

He looked through one of the windows at a shared area in the middle of the complex. There were patio chairs and small barbecues grills. Then he gauged the distance between the apartments. *No way*, he thought, *someone could barge into one of these apartments and shoot up the place without someone seeing or hearing something. But there's a difference between seeing or hearing something and telling the police about it.* "Does the complex have security cameras?" he asked.

"Just installed," she answered.

He opened the closet in the smaller bedroom, wondering how Lakisha had hidden herself inside without being found, especially if the robbers were there to steal drugs and cash. He wondered why he'd come here. None of that really mattered. He blamed Adrian Wilson for setting in motion the events that had led to all of this. Mookie was right. Wilson needed to pay. He turned his attention back to the agent in mid-sentence.

"The lease is for thirteen months, one thousand, seven hundred ninety-five dollars per month," she said.

"Sounds good," he said.

"Mr. Winslow, it looks like Two-H might be available," she noted. "Would you like me to get those keys?"

"No," he answered. "Think I've seen enough."

Chapter 25

Joey seemed proud of her work as she held a small, homemade card in front of her. A thin, black and white ribbon was strung from top to bottom at one end of the square card; an image of a large tree was centered on black and white card stock, which was framed by red. She handed her creation to Rasheeda.

"Think it's okay?" she asked.

Rasheeda eyeballed the greeting card and then slowly read the words inside: "I really appreciate your help the other day. You rescued me from a tight spot. I will forever be grateful for your assistance. Thanks again, Joey."

Rasheeda looked closely at the card again and handed it back to Joey. "You make this?" she asked.

"Yes, I did," Joey answered proudly.

"Wouldn't it have been easier to buy one from the store?"

"Yes, it would have been."

"Then why go through the trouble?"

Joey shook her head in disbelief. "It's important to thank people properly," she insisted.

Rasheeda played with her hair. "Is that a thank you or an invitation?" she asked. "Hard for me to tell."

"Please," Joey responded.

"Didn't you say thank you after he switched your tire?"

"Yes, I did. But when someone goes out of their way to help you out, that deserves more than a verbal thank you."

Rasheeda smiled. "So we *are* talking about the same thing?"

"Get your mind out the gutter," Joey urged. She walked over and sat next to Rasheeda on her bed. "Let me tell you a story."

"Do you have to?" Rasheeda asked.

"It's not a long story," Joey explained. "One year my brother and I both received Christmas cards from one of my aunts. Each card had ten dollars in it."

"Was it a fancy homemade card or a dime-store card?"

"I don't remember," Joey answered, shaking her head. "What does that have to do with anything? Anyhow, I wrote a thank-you note. My brother didn't. The next year, we both got cards again. Thing is, my card had twenty dollars in it. My brother didn't get anything."

"You think your aunt forgot to put money in your brother's card?"

"No," Joey surmised. "I'm guessing he didn't get any money because he never acknowledged the ten dollars he'd gotten the year before. Would you keep sending gifts to someone who doesn't thank you?"

Rasheeda pondered the story for a moment. "So you want Christian to keep doing things for you?" she asked.

"No."

"Did you share the twenty dollars with your brother?"

"No."

Chapter 26

As he sat in the waiting room at the social services office, Tobias rehearsed his answers while periodically checking the clock on the wall. There were no logical answers to the questions Lakisha would likely ask. Still, he thought it better to anticipate as many of her questions as possible.

How come my dad never mentioned you?

Well, I'm guessing he didn't know that I was his father. I'm guessing your grandmother never told him who his father was. He probably didn't know I existed. Don't mean to talk bad 'bout your grandmother. I'm sure she did what she had to do. Can't do anything 'bout that now.

How come you didn't tell him?

Wasn't anything to tell. That your grandmother was pregnant, that she was carrying my child, this is all news to me. This is as much a surprise to me as it is to you. I'm still trying to wrap my head 'round it.

How could you not know?

Well, the truth is I was in prison. The only thing I was focused on at that time was surviving each day in the pen. If you focus on anything else when you're away, you won't make it. Never heard from your grandmother while I was doing time. Not that I tried to contact her either. When I got out, never saw or heard of Sugar. Not till a couple of weeks ago. That's what I called your grandmother, Sugar.

Why are you here now?

Not sure. I've found out that I had a son. That he had a daughter. My granddaughter. You. Ain't never had a son or a grandchild before. I have no idea where to start as far as being a grandfather. At times, I'm happy. Most times, I'm mad. More like scared, I guess. Everything in me wants to strike out at those who put me in this situation. Where should I start? It's like someone took something away from me. Only thing is, how can someone take something from you that you never knew you had? I realize that don't make much sense.

Why were you in prison? You sell drugs like my father?

That don't matter anymore. Did my time and never looked back. Got my barber's license while I was in prison. Have owned my own shop for three decades. I did something that was wrong. And I had to pay for it—

"Mr. Winslow."

The receptionist at the agency interrupted Tobias' thoughts. He followed her down a hallway to the meeting room. It was a short walk, but it seemed like the longest walk of his life. His heartbeat increased, and he struggled to breathe.

Inside the meeting room, a middle-aged man and woman sat on a couch on either side of a young girl. Donna sat in a chair facing the couch. The girl was tall and slender, with well-defined cheekbones like her grandmother. She appeared more mature than in any of the photos Tobias had seen.

Tobias felt faint as he entered the room. He placed his hand on the back of a chair and steadied himself. Donna was speaking, but he didn't really hear or understand anything she said. His eyes filled with tears as he held himself up against the chair. He looked to Donna for assistance as he felt himself losing consciousness.

The young girl got up from the couch and rushed over to him. She put her arms around him in a tight embrace. He stood frozen, trying desperately to catch his breath and hold himself up.

Chapter 27

Christian paced back and forth in his dorm room, rehearsing his speech for class. The music playing in the background didn't bother him. Rather, he used it to help him establish pace and tone. When he heard a knock, he wasn't sure whether it was part of the music or someone at his door. When he opened his door to check, Joey pushed past him, carrying a small cake and an envelope.

"Come in, why don't you?" he said, motioning her in with one arm. "What's this?"

She sat the cake on top of the scattered papers on his desk. He used a remote to turn down the music.

"A little thank you," she said, smiling. She handed the envelope to him. "Open it," she urged.

He opened the envelope and carefully examined the card. He admired the stenciling, and the coordinated color pattern. It looked like the fancy invitations sent for weddings or baby showers. "You make this?"

"Yes." She beamed. "You like it?"

"It's very nice," he complimented. "But it really wasn't necessary. And the cake?"

"Bought that. Afraid I'm not very good in the kitchen," she admitted. "Hope you like red velvet."

"Sure do." He glanced at the books spread across his bed. "I was sort of in the middle of studying for an exam," he explained. "Really need to get back to that."

"Oh," she said. "I'm sorry. I didn't mean to interrupt. Just wanted to say thank you, that's all. I'll let you get back to your studying."

He looked to the door.

"There *is* one other thing," she hinted.

"Something else?"

"Yes. I saw that you're scheduled for a late tutoring session next week at the rec center. I'd be happy to cover that for you."

He looked down and laughed. "This is tearing you apart, isn't it?" he asked.

"What?"

"I do something for you, so you have to do something for me. Is that how it works in your world?"

"Something wrong with that?"

"Guess not," he said, looking at the cake. "Works for me. Though it seems a lot easier to simply accept the gesture, say thanks, and move on. I'm good with the tutoring session, though. But thanks for the offer."

"Well, okay," she said, turning to leave.

"There *is* one thing you could do for me," he said.

She stood in the doorway with her back turned to him. "What would that be?" she asked, smiling and turning toward him. "Need help studying?"

"No, I've got that covered. Saturday," he said. "Meet me in the parking lot around nine in the morning."

"Saturday."

"Yes."

"In the student parking lot."

"At nine a.m.," he repeated. "Might take a few hours, though."

"Well, okay," she agreed.

Chapter 28

"Next."

The corrections officer at the Los Angeles Detention Center motioned Tobias toward a vacant video monitor. Tobias sat in the chair in front of the monitor and read the instructions posted next to the small screen. He fed a ten-dollar bill into the cash slot. Then he input the inmate number he'd been given during the visitation check-in. The name "Khalilah Daniels" flashed on the monitor's screen, followed by the words "stand by."

After a few minutes, a stop clock set to fifteen minutes appeared on the screen and began winding down. Then a disheveled-looking woman appeared. Her prison-issued glasses were held together by masking tape. Her dark hair went in every direction, and colorful tattoos rose from her uniform collar to her chin.

"Do I know you?" the woman asked.

"Are you Khalilah Daniels?"

"Yes."

"I'm Tobias Winslow. I'm here to talk to you about your daughter, Lakisha."

"What about her?"

"I'm Elton's father. From Cleveland," Tobias stated. "I'm here to settle his affairs and see that Lakisha is placed in a suitable home."

Khalilah wiped sweat from her forehead with a small washcloth. "Sorry to hear 'bout your son," she said. "He was a good man. Best baby daddy I've ever had. That's for sure."

"Thanks. About Lakisha—do you have other children?"

"Got five. Three boys, two girls." She paused and then began counting with her fingers. "No," she corrected. "Six. Why do you ask?"

"I was wondering who's taking care of them. Wondering if they could look after Lakisha as well. Probably be best that siblings be together. You think?"

"You ain't got to worry 'bout them," she explained. "State done took them away and put them up for adoption. Said I was an unfit mother. Believe that? They'll take care of Kisha, too."

"Thing is, they want me to take her back to Cleveland. Make a home for her there. I'm not sure that's the right thing. Not sure I can care for her. And I'm sure you'd want her to stay in LA?"

Khalilah tossed her hands into the air. "Why are you bringing this to me? What do you want me to do?" she asked. "Tell them you can't take care of her. Or you don't want to. They'll find a place for her."

"I was hoping we could come up with some temporary solution, at least 'til you get out," he countered. "Then you could take care of your daughter. I'm sure that's what you want."

"Kisha will be legal by the time I get outta here," she noted. "Ain't nothing I can do for her. She don't need no junkie mother, anyway."

Tobias noticed the time flashing on the monitor. He had eight more minutes. He couldn't imagine what more he could say to Khalilah that would take eight minutes, couldn't imagine spending another minute with her without losing his patience. She didn't resemble the woman in the photos he'd seen. He doubted Elton or anyone else would be interested in her, had they'd initially seen this side of her. She reminded him of the women who panhandled near the women's shelter in downtown Cleveland.

"Lakisha's been through a lot," he continued. "I'm thinking that being with people she's familiar with might help."

"Mr. Winslow, I'm sorry 'bout your son. Really am," she said. "But right now, I got to do me. I don't need you stressing me out. Putting things on my mind that I can't do nothing 'bout. Ain't nothing I can do for Kisha. She better off without me. I'm fighting to get clean. Survive this place. You ever been locked up? You have any clue what it's like in here?"

He didn't answer. Instead, he placed the receiver

down and got up from the chair. She waved one hand furiously to get him to pick the receiver back up. He reluctantly lifted it back to his ear.

"Think you could put a few dollars on my account 'fore you leave?" she asked. "Help a sister out?"

Chapter 29

Joey stared at the ranch-style home that Christian parked next to on the street. A lone rocking chair sat on the small porch on the front of the house, the lawn was meticulously manicured, and a light breeze rocked the welcome sign protruding from the garden next to the porch.

"Where are we?" she asked, finally.

Christian reached into the small storage compartment between the front seats of his car and retrieved a pair of work gloves and sunglasses.

"You'll see," he answered.

As they exited his car, a little boy and girl ran out of the front door of the home straight toward Christian. McKenzie Frazier followed closely behind. Christian reached out, grabbed the little girl, and lifted her into the air.

"Whatcha gonna be?" he asked, playfully tickling her as he did. "Whatcha gonna be?"

"A doctor!" the girl shouted. "And a singer."

"That's what I'm talkin' 'bout," he blurted out. He turned his attention to the little boy, grabbing him. "Whatcha gonna be? Whatcha gonna be?"

The boy covered his mouth with his hands, smiled, and looked away.

"Whatcha gonna be?" Christian repeated. "Whatcha gonna be?"

"He doesn't know," the little girl interjected.

"That's okay," Christian assured. "He's got plenty of time. Daija, Cordell, say hello to Miss Joey."

"Hello," they said in unison before running back into the house. Kenzie embraced Christian.

"You working today?" he asked.

"Yes," she replied. "Mom's going to watch them till I get back."

Kenzie extended her hand to Joey.

"I'm McKenzie," she said. "Christian's cousin."

"Joey. Nice to meet you."

"Wish I could stay," Kenzie said. "But I'm late for work."

Joey followed Christian into the home. Madeline Dubois stood in the dining room staring out the window. Cordell and Daija tugged at her dress.

"Aunt Maddie," Christian called out. "Brought you some company this morning. Didn't know you already had some."

Maddie diverted her attention from the scene outside her window to her two grandchildren.

"What are you two fussing about?" she asked.

They pointed to Christian.

"Hello, Christian," Maddie said. "When'd you get here?"

"Just did, Aunt Maddie," he answered. "This is Joey, a friend from college. Thought I'd bring you a little company."

"Why come on in, young lady," Maddie directed. "Have a seat. About to get myself some coffee. Can I get you a cup?"

"Sure," Joey replied. "Why not?"

"Daija. Cordell, you treat Miss Joey nice," Christian instructed. He looked at Joey. "I'll be outside if you need me."

She gave him a puzzled look as he left. *Are you serious*, she thought? *You going to introduce me to some strangers and then disappear?*

Outside, he got a ladder from the garage and propped it up against one side of the home. He scaled the ladder and began pulling leaves and debris from the gutters. He methodically moved around the home until he'd removed all the leaves. He peered through a window as he lifted a water hose to the gutter to rinse it. Joey sat across from Aunt Maddie, who was pointing out photos in a large album. Cordell and Daija were huddled on each side of Joey on the floor. Maddie pointed to a photo of a home surrounded by a vast field that seemed to stretch forever.

"I lived there for years," she revealed. "Right up 'til the time I moved north. Go back down once or twice a year. Land's been in my family for decades."

"Why'd you move north?" Joey asked.

"After my husband died, I had a couple of falls. Kenzie, my daughter, thought it'd be better if I lived closer," Maddie answered. "And I get to see my grand-children more often."

The sound of a small engine revving up interrupted Joey's thoughts. She looked out the window and saw Christian blowing leaves into the street with a portable leaf blower. He then swept debris from the driveway. Inside, Maddie dozed off. Joey read several books to Daija and Cordell. She was about to start another when Christian came back into the house.

"Aunt Maddie," he called.

"Huh?" she responded, waking from her brief nap. "You ready for some lunch?"

"Rain check," he said. "Need to be getting back to the school. Few more things I need to do today."

"Boy, you can't never sit still," Maddie commented. "Always running. That's what your mother used to always say."

Christian grabbed Daija. "Whatcha gonna be?" he asked, tickling her. "Whatcha gonna be?"

"Told you already," she answered. "You forget already?"

He grabbed Cordell. "Whatcha gonna be? Whatcha gonna be?"

"A lawyer," Cordell answered. "A lawyer."

Christian looked at Joey. She smiled.

"Good," he said. "May be needing your services one day."

ↁↂↁ

"Exactly how did I help you?" Joey asked as Christian was driving back to the university.

"All those photos you saw. All those stories you heard. If I had to hear them all over again, for the hundredth or so time, it would've taken me twice as long to get that work done," he explained. "And with Daija and Cordell, I would've been there 'til dinner."

"Glad I could help," she said. "But it was really my pleasure. Your aunt is fascinating. She's lived such a full life. And those cousins of yours are precious."

"They are."

"Do you visit her every weekend?"

"Not every weekend," he said. "I try to get over at least every few. That way I can take care of the yard work. Or sit and talk with her for a while. She likes to talk."

Chapter 30

Eric Washington was unloading a truck near the rear entrance of a fast-food restaurant in South Central LA when Tobias found him. He'd been Lakisha's social worker prior to Donna, and she thought he could provide some useful insights about both Elton and Lakisha.

"Mr. Washington?"

Eric looked up from his clipboard at Tobias. "Yes," he answered. "Can I help you, sir?"

"I'm Tobias Winslow. Donna Brennan thought it would be a good idea if I spoke with you."

Eric smiled. "Donna's good people," he commented. "Definitely someone you can trust. But like I've told her numerous times, I'm done with all of that. Retired from social work. So no, I'm not interested in anything you're offering. I'm content doing this job until I get my teaching certificate."

Tobias retrieved a cigarette from his pack and extended the pack to Eric.

"Thanks," Eric said, taking one.

"I'm not here offering a job, Mr. Washington. I was hoping to get some information about my son and granddaughter—Elton Davis and Lakisha Daniels."

Eric froze momentarily and then placed his clipboard down. "I'm sorry for your loss, Mr. Winslow. My condolences. What a tragedy. I'm not really supposed to talk about my cases. But I'm not employed by the county anymore. So how can I help you?"

Tobias extended his lit cigarette. Eric used it to light his.

"How long were you involved in the case?" Tobias asked.

"Going back two, three years," Eric said. "Picked up the file after Lakisha and her siblings were removed from her mother's home. The case worker who had it was fired for poor supervision."

"What happened?"

"Khalilah and her kids were living in a rented house. We were going through a heat wave and there were no working air conditioners in the home. The case worker, she used petty cash to get some window units for the home."

"They gave cash to a dope fiend?"

Eric exhaled smoke.

"Of course not," he answered. "You think we're clueless? We bought the units directly from the store.

Hired a handyman to install them. The caseworker's mistake was not checking back for several days."

"And?"

"When she checked back a week or so later, the children were unsupervised in the home—and several of them were suffering from heat stroke and had to be hospitalized. There was no food in the home, and there was cat and dog feces all over the place."

"Heat stroke? What about the air conditioners?"

"Khalilah and her crackhead boyfriend had removed the air-conditioning units and pawned them. If you know anything about social services, you know that someone had to be blamed other than the people directly responsible. Doesn't matter that the case worker probably had thirty ongoing cases, half of them on emergency status. The case worker was fired, the children were placed in foster homes, and that's how Lakisha's file landed on my desk."

Tobias shook his head. "We can't pick our parents, can we?" he lamented.

"Believe it or not, things started looking up for Lakisha at that point. Elton had recently been released from county on a drug case. He agreed to take parenting courses, and we were able to eventually place Lakisha with him. He loved that girl. He made sure she was at school every day, made sure she was clothed and fed, and tried to keep her away from her mother's family. And she was excelling in school. Her teachers loved her."

"Tell me about Elton."

"He wasn't a *bad* young man, but he made *bad*

choices. The constant pull of the street hustle kept calling his name, and he kept answering it. It's that way for some young men. They fully understand that they ought to go in a different direction, but the pull of the streets can be too strong sometimes, even when it doesn't make sense to follow it."

"Why you think that is?"

"Best I can figure? Even for young men and women following the straight-and-narrow, when something happens that disrupts their lives, they feel as though they've wasted time investing in a system that wasn't designed for them, that's rejected them over and over. Then they turn to their own devices—whether that's a quick way to make money or to settle a dispute." Eric took a deep drag. "I was able to get Elton into a construction trade apprenticeship. He stuck with it for about a month," he said. "But there was no way he was going to haul around construction materials for six days and get a check at the end of the week for less than he'd make in a day selling weed."

"He sold weed, nothing harder?"

"That's hard enough, Mr. Winslow. More people are killed involved with weed than all the other drugs. Anybody looking for easy cash knows who'll have some weed *and* cash—the neighborhood weed dealer. And often innocent people around the weed dealer are caught in the crossfire."

"He was a good father?"

"He wasn't in line for any awards, if that's what you're asking. He did the best he could. He called me several times to bail him out of small problems. And he always said he'd do right by the girl. He was always straight with me."

Tobias explained that hadn't known Elton or Lakisha, about the predicament he now found himself in, and that he wasn't sure he was prepared to raise Lakisha, or if it would be best to take her away from Los Angeles and her family. "Do you think it would be harmful to uproot her?" he asked Eric.

Eric extinguished his cigarette. "Mr. Winslow, I can't imagine what it would be like to be in your shoes, to learn about your son and granddaughter in such a horrible way," he said. "But if you care anything about Lakisha, if you even think you might grow to care anything about her, you'll get her as far away from here as possible. She can't survive this place."

Chapter 31

Christian didn't immediately greet Joey when she entered the break room at the recreation center. Instead, he continued staring into his textbook. She was smiling as she sat down across from him, anxious to discuss Maddie and his cousins.

"I would've never guessed you're from Louisiana," she started.

"I'm not from Louisiana," he replied, matter-of-factly. "Lived in Cleveland all my life."

"Your people," Joey responded. "Your aunt said your family roots are in Louisiana."

"Guess so," he reluctantly acknowledged. "I've been there once or twice. I don't own any of the backward stuff, though."

She paused and stared at him. "You saying folks from Louisiana are backward?"

"What would you call it—cutting off chicken's heads and gathering in the woods to chant unintelligent things, all while downing moonshine someone made in their shed?"

"I'm from Louisiana," she informed him.

"No, you're not," he retorted. "I heard you telling Mrs. Scott that you're from Houston. Isn't that what you said the other day?"

"My family lives in Houston now," she explained. "But I grew up in Louisiana. Lived there until I was eight or nine."

He sipped his coffee. "Why did your family leave?" he asked.

"The backwoods you mean?"

He cringed with embarrassment. "Sorry about that," he offered.

"Hurricane Katrina. You may have heard of it?" she said sarcastically. "Most of my extended family still lives in Louisiana. We got relocated after the hurricane. And my family decided to stay in Houston."

"Sorry to hear that."

"I plan to go back one day."

He shook his head. "Why?"

"Because it's where I'm from. And some of those backward people you're talking about, some are related to me. You too, apparently. We might be related. for all you know."

"I'm definitely not seeing that."

"Anyway, I wanted to ask you something."

"What?"

"Your aunt," she continued. "I think she'd be a great speaker for our young black women's group at school. She told me that she trained black teachers and traveled throughout the South, helping people set up schools. And that society she created is fascinating."

"Oh," he said. "She told you about that?"

"Why wouldn't she? I'd love to go to one of those society meetings. I could pretend that I'm connected. Or you could take me."

"That isn't going to happen," he stated. "I don't have any time for those meetings. Every once in a while, though, she does presentations at the libraries around here on Louisiana black history. You'd enjoy them."

"You think she'd be interested in speaking to our women's group?"

"She'd probably like that," he admitted. "As I've said, she loves to talk. But don't expect her to talk about cutting off chicken heads or that voodoo stuff."

Joey stood. "For someone in college," she scolded, "you say some pretty ignorant things."

❧❧❧

The westerly breeze off the ocean provided a reprieve from the day's oppressive heat, and that persuaded Tobias to open the windows in his hotel room and shut off the air conditioner. He wished he was back home in Cleveland, where the breeze off Lake Erie on many summer nights made it bearable to sleep without the manufactured chill from a machine, even if he had to use his squeaky attic fan to jumpstart the air flow. The LA breeze, however unexpected, felt good, but the sound of cars whizzing past was obtrusive. He'd gotten used to the attic fan. But this sound was something else.

Tobias retrieved one of the DVDs Donna had given him and slid it into the DVD player. The first part of the recording was a grainy picture over which a woman's voice could be heard. He reached out to push the eject button, but the grain and noise dissipated, and he decided to allow the DVD to continue to play.

When the picture and sound became clear, Lakisha was sitting at a backyard table. She wore an oversized sweatshirt and jeans. Her hair was pulled behind her head and tied with a multicolored ribbon. Someone had placed a smiley-face sticker on one of her cheeks.

To one side of her, there was a small toy stove and a play tea set. On her other side were several mounds of play dough. The woman who could be heard on the recording began asking questions.

"What is this, Lakisha?" the woman asked, as the camera zoomed in on the stove and play set.

"It's my kitchen," Lakisha answered.

"And what are you making today?"

"Turkey and cranberry sauce and stuffing. And everyone's coming over for dinner, including my dad."

"Any dessert?"

"Ice cream. And pie."

"That sounds delicious. Can I come?"

Lakisha smiled, but didn't answer.

Most likely, the woman asking the questions was a social worker or child psychologist. Tobias could faintly hear other children's voices in the background. And when the camera changed angles, he could see they were at a daycare, or at least some place with plenty of children's play equipment.

The camera zoomed in on the mounds of play dough—one mound was yellow, another was red, and the third was blue.

"And what are these?" the woman asked.

"This is my house," Lakisha explained.

"Can you please tell me what each thing is?"

Lakisha pointed to the red structure. "This is the house. Like I said."

"Okay, what about the yellow?"

"That's the garage."

"And the blue?"

"That's the pool. You need to have a pool 'cause sometimes it gets too hot in the house. And you can go swimming if you can't walk to the beach."

Chapter 32

Donna and Tobias stood near one of the departure boards at LAX. The words "on time" flashed in green next to his scheduled flight to Cleveland. He hated flying, but he'd never been happier to board a plane. Every mile separating him from Los Angeles would be welcomed.

"I'll be calling you in the next week or so, Mr. Winslow," Donna said. "As soon as we finalize a date for Lakisha to visit."

"Okay," he replied.

"You'll also be hearing from Cuyahoga County Family Services. They're going to want to arrange a home visit and inspection. You'll want to handle that right away."

"Okay," he repeated.

"They'll also finish the process of putting a team of support people in place. A child psychologist, an academic counselor, a primary care physician," she added.

"Will you be coming out with her?"

"Not sure if it will be me or someone else," she answered. "But she'll definitely have a traveling companion."

She handed him a file.

"What's this?" he asked.

"It's an old address for Kendall's sister," she said. "Probably be a good idea to make contact with Sugar's family."

He gave her a puzzled look.

"If Sugar has siblings still alive, then Lakisha has cousins, aunts, uncles living near you," she speculated. "They could provide a bit more support for you."

"I wouldn't know what to say to them," he confided.

"Tell them the truth," Donna said. "Sugar has a granddaughter."

"What would I tell them about me?" he asked. "They don't know me from Adam. Don't you think that would be awkward?"

"There's a lot that's awkward about this situation, Mr. Winslow," she conceded. "My only concern is creating a structure that will support Lakisha. If Sugar's people can be part of the solution, then so be it."

Chapter 33

Maddie's house seemed eerily silent without Daija and Cordell there. Standing on a ladder, Christian tossed the container that held the light bulbs onto the dining-room table below him then carefully lifted the globe to the lighting fixture into place and secured it tightly. He smiled as he recalled Joey playing with his cousins a few feet away. She could be annoying at times, but he couldn't deny that he was rapidly warming to her.

He admired the ease with which she handled children—whether it was his cousins or those at the recreation program. There didn't seem to be a situation where she was out of place.

He didn't always appreciate her approach, but the things she said usually made sense.

He eased himself off the stepladder as Maddie stood silently at the window.

"Why do you keep staring out that window?" he asked.

Maddie didn't answer.

"Aunt Maddie?"

"Huh?"

"What's so interesting outside? You've been staring out that window all morning."

She walked away from the dining room window to the kitchen. "Worried about that tree branch," she said. "Every time the wind gets to howling, I can hear it creaking and cracking. Afraid, it's going to break off and come crashing down on my roof. Or come down when Daija or Cordell are out there playing."

He walked over to window and peered out.

"Yeah, that does look a bit suspect," he said. "I'll tell you what, the next time Sebastian's over I'll have him hold the ladder for me, and I'll go up and take care of it with the chain saw. Wouldn't feel comfortable going up that high on a ladder unless I have someone making sure it can't move on me."

"Oh, that sounds good," she said. "I hope it doesn't come down before you get to it."

"Next week," he said. "I promise."

There was a knock at the front door.

Christian was surprised at the sight of Joey standing outside.

"Hey! It's Miss Joey," Maddie announced, as she made her way to the door. She looked back at Christian. "You didn't tell me you were expecting company."

"I wasn't," Christian noted.

Maddie unlatched the door and ushered Joey in. "Come on in," she urged. "Christian's in the dining room."

"Actually, I'm here to see you, Mrs. Dubois," Joey stressed. "I wanted to invite you to speak to our young black women's group at school. Don't think it's fair that only your family gets to hear about all of your wonderful experiences. And all those things you and your daughter are involved with. They need to be shared with others." Joey glared at Christian. "*Some* people appreciate the past," she commented.

Maddie smiled as she embraced Joey's hand. "You're so kind," Maddie said. "So nice of you to think of me. I think I would enjoy that. Of course, I would have to find someone to give me a ride. Kenzie wouldn't like me driving that far."

"That can be arranged," Joey asserted. She placed several papers on the coffee table. "This is some information about the group and the dates that we meet. You can look at this when you have time, and if any of these dates work for you, call me and I'll schedule it."

"I sure will," Maddie promised. "It's been a while since I spoke at a college. But if you don't mind an old woman rambling, I could probably still muddle through. Can you stay for coffee or tea?"

"I wish I could," Joey said, looking back over at Christian. "But I have a ton of things to do back at school. I'll show myself out."

Christian followed her out the door to her car. He placed his hand on the door handle before she could get in, and she turned toward him.

She glanced at his hand. "Is there something you wanted?"

"I wanted to apologize for the other day at the rec center," he said. "I shouldn't have said those things. You were right. They were ignorant things to say."

"They were," she said.

"We've gotten off to a bad start," he said. "I'm hoping we can get past that."

"We'll see."

Chapter 34

Marcel worked on a customer. Cameron sat in his chair and read the newspaper. Antonio Cochran, dressed in a double-breasted suit and silk tie, stood near the entryway to the beauty shop holding a bouquet. Chante emerged and greeted him.

"These for me?" she asked, smiling.

"Of course," Antonio replied.

"Thanks."

Antonio kissed Chante on her cheek.

"I wasn't expecting you this morning, Antonio," she observed. "Something else you need to give me?"

"No, no," he said. "I got up this morning and decided I wanted to lay eyes on you. Start my day out right."

She blushed.

"When am I going to see you again?" he inquired.

"Why don't you give me a call and set something

up?" she suggested. "Can't talk now—I've got customers waiting."

He pulled her close and tried to kiss her again, but she turned away.

"Not here," she calmly protested.

He turned and walked to the front door, smiling at her as he did. "Looking forward to the day we're partners," he commented.

As Antonio exited the shop, Tobias entered. He paused in the doorway to let Antonio pass and to remove the ticket taped to the door. Then he walked over to Marcel's station.

"Good morning, Mr. Winslow," Marcel said.

"Morning," Tobias replied. "Got any change?"

"What do you need?"

"Two twenties and a ten will do."

Marcel handed him fifty dollars. Tobias handed Marcel the ticket.

"What's this?" Marcel asked.

"I believe that's yours, son," Tobias said.

"What is it?"

"It's the fifty-dollar ticket I got this morning 'cause you didn't sweep the front sidewalk."

Cameron laughed.

"That ain't right," Marcel objected. "It's your ticket, why don't you pay it?"

"We've been through this, son," Tobias reminded him. "First thing you do on Tuesdays is sweep the sidewalk. Sidewalk don't get swept, I get a ticket."

"What's that got to do with me?" Marcel asked. "It's your shop. That don't seem fair."

Cameron interjected. "Marcel, didn't I remind you to sweep the sidewalk this morning? Right after you hung up your coat?" he asked.

Did he? Marcel asked himself.

Chante emerged from the beauty shop. "Shame on you, Tobias," she said. She taped a task list next to Marcel's station. "You need to check this list every day," she instructed Marcel. "Right after you get in. Before you take your first customer."

Marcel looked at the list. "That's a good idea," he acknowledged.

Tobias glanced at the clock on the wall and then turned on the television. He found the channel he wanted and then turned it back off. Then he positioned two pieces of construction paper on the floor in the middle of the shop, one white and one black, and placed thirty dollars on the black sheet.

"Anybody want any of this?" Tobias asked.

Cameron placed twenty dollars on the black.

"That's fifty dollars on the line," Tobias announced, glancing at the few people in the shop.

Chante dropped twenty dollars on the white sheet.

"One minute to air time," Tobias advised.

"How does this work?" Marcel asked.

Tobias looked up at the television. "The news is 'bout to start," he began. "If you think the first criminal they 'bout to show us is black, then put your money on the black sheet. Put it on white if you think otherwise. Winners collect the pot and divide it."

Marcel dropped twenty dollars on the white sheet.

"It's on!" Tobias declared. "It's on!"

He turned the television back on and waited. After a brief weather update, and a recap of the latest Browns loss, the news anchor read the first crime story.

"Today, there are two arrests following reports of a sixteen-year-old found dead in a Parma motel room," the anchor began. "Police believe the teenager died of a hero-in overdose. The teen's mother and grandmother are now in custody, suspected of supplying the lethal drugs."

Photos of the mother and grandmother appeared on the screen.

"Oh, no, don't do it to me," Tobias fretted. "Say it ain't so!"

Marcel playfully broke into a dance near his work-station. Chante collected the money, glared at Tobias, then handed the fifty dollars to Marcel.

Chapter 35

S o why'd you pick this place?"

On the third Wednesday of each month, Tobias and Cameron attended an invitation-only poker game at a condo near Shaker Square—with other barbers, sanitation workers, landscapers, and various blue-collar workers who really couldn't afford to lose fifty to one hundred dollars, but did so regularly. Usually, they stopped some place for a sit-down meal before arriving at the card game by eight p.m. The doors closed sharply at that time, and anyone late had to wait for the next go around the next month. Since it was Tobias's turn to select a place to eat, he chose Sebastian's Place because it was close to the poker game and he wanted to check it out.

Neither he nor Cameron had ever been to Sebastian's and the crowd it attracted—young, black and white professionals, a few artistic types, and folks from the upscale residences in walking distance—made them feel a little out of place. Most of the other patrons hovered near the bar. Tobias and Cameron found a table in one corner of the room as far away from the bar patrons as possible.

"This is my cousin's place," Tobias answered, explaining his selection.

"Your cousin? You ain't got no cousin who owns no restaurant," Cameron commented. "You lying to me."

Tobias looked up from his plate. "The one who stopped by the shop—after he saw that sticker in the window. You heard what he said—if my Aunt Bessie is a Dreamer, then so am I. We're family."

"Whatever, man," Cameron said, shaking his head. "This *is* a nice place though. Didn't know that you liked Cajun."

"Didn't know it myself 'til I had it done the right way at that park. Man, that was some good food! Must've gone back for two, three helpings."

Cameron laughed. "I believe the helpings part," he said. "You tend to overdo it at times."

Sebastian arrived at their table. "So how are your meals?" he inquired.

"This is great, really good," Cameron praised. "And this is some place you've got here."

"Perfect," Tobias added.

Sebastian smiled. "That's what I like to hear." He focused on Tobias. "Do you remember the woman on stage at the park—the one who did most of the talking and explained the stickers?" Sebastian asked.

"Yeah. Yeah. Guess I do."

"That's my wife. She's not here tonight, or I'd certainly introduce her. But I plan to stop by your shop one day so you can meet her. She loves to meet Dreamers. It's becoming her second job."

"That'd be great," Tobias said. "And anytime you need a trim or a shave, you know where to stop."

Sebastian looked back toward the kitchen. "If I can do anything else for you gentlemen don't hesitate," he smiled. "And your money's no good tonight."

"Why thank you," Tobias said. Tobias looked straight at Cameron as Sebastian left. "So you think I'm doing the right thing?" he asked.

"I think you're doing the *mature* thing," Cameron answered. "Right now, your focus needs to be on your granddaughter. You've got to let the rest of that stuff go. It'll kill you, one way or another."

"That's easy to say," Tobias explained, a stern, more-serious look replacing his smile. "If you had seen that apartment. That scene. And imagined that girl hiding in a closet while her father was being murdered. Don't seem right that no one has paid."

"Who do you think should pay? And what can you do 'bout it?"

"The only person I can make pay is Adrian Wilson. I can't do anything 'bout what happened in LA. But I can handle the Cleveland part. It ain't right that someone can set things in motion and then walk away and watch folks fend for themselves. Wash their hands of the whole thing."

Cameron shook his head. "It's the American way," he responded. "Toby, the person that's paying is your granddaughter. And she'll have to pay even more if you go and do something stupid, get yourself put away again. Do you want to be back up in the pen with Mookie? Want to die behind bars? You walked away from that years ago. Do you really want to go back to that life?"

Tobias exhaled. "You right. You right," he affirmed. "But I feel like I need to do something."

"Let it go," Cameron said, calmly. "And every time you sense your anger growing, take a deep breath."

"Let it go?"

"Yes, bury it."

Chapter 36

Dee—" Christian said. "Dee—"

Deante Walker looked up from the stool in the garage bay. Slowly, he lifted his body and began wheeling a tire toward the car hoisted on a jack in the driveway on which Christian stood. When he wasn't running numbers, D-man worked at his uncle's used tire shop south of Interstate 480 in Maple Heights. It was a good place to lie low when needed. It was also where he and Christian had worked on weekends throughout high school. He leaned toward Christian and embraced him.

"'Sup nigga?"

"Everything's cool. You, D-man?"

"I'm good."

Christian slipped twenty dollars into D-man's front shirt pocket.

"What's this?"

"It's for that tire you fixed for me a couple of weeks

back. You didn't think I was wasting any money on the numbers, did you?"

Deante smiled. "If you'd bet with your head, and not your heart, you might win a few bucks. I mean, who bets on the Browns anyway, unless it's to lose?"

"Yeah, you got that."

Deante held the bills in his hand. "Sure you don't need to keep this for yourself? Don't you need this to pay for that school?" he asked. "At least one of us needs to get an education and follow the straight and narrow. Don't think it's gonna be me."

Christian laughed. "No, it's yours. It's not from me," Christian informed him. "That student I told you about— she insisted on giving me some money for taking care of the tire. Not like I could keep it. You did the work. I just hadn't had the time to come back and give it to you before now."

D-man kneeled down and lifted the repaired tire onto the car in the driveway. "We should hangout sometime— like the old days," D-man suggested.

"Maybe," Christian answered. "Maybe."

They both knew "maybe" most likely meant never. While they'd been close throughout high school—played on sports teams together and had once gone to the same church—it was rare that they saw each other these days. They ran in different circles. Christian identified with the up-and-coming young African Americans who were increasingly becoming more involved politically and challenging the city's old black guard, Deante with those who'd long since decided the system was corrupt, regardless of whether the figurehead out front was black or white, and that any gain for them would have to be forcibly taken.

Christian avoided the dangerous clubs and bars they'd once frequented throughout the eastside—places where young black men settled disputes with weapons. Deante felt most comfortable in those places. They served as his bases of operation for hustling and entertainment.

Their unofficial parting of the ways happened during the summer after Christian's first year at FDU, when Deante and two others riding in stolen car spotted Christian walking along Euclid Avenue. The trio picked him up and were cruising across East 55th Street when a police car pulled them over.

One by one, the officers removed them from the car and placed them against the side of a building. A subsequent search of the car found a small amount of marijuana under a seat and on two of the occupants—and Deante had an outstanding warrant. As one of the officers searched Christian, he removed his FDU student ID from his back pocket. The ID noted that Christian was an Urban Scholar recipient. The police officer put the ID back into Christian's wallet and then tossed the wallet down the sidewalk.

"Why'd you do that?" Christian demanded. "What's your problem?"

"My problem is wanna-be gangsters like you who hook up this these street punks," the officer said. "My problem is young black men who are too stupid to see they're throwing their lives away." The officer pointed down the street. "You see that RTA bus heading this way?" he asked. "You're going to pick up your wallet and get on that bus. Not the next one, and not one coming in a direct direction. And I better not see your black ass again. Understand? If I do, I'm going to slap the taste out your mouth."

Christian stood defiant, staring at the officer's dark brown eyes, his mahogany skin.

"Do you understand English?" the officer asked. "Or would you prefer to go downtown with these hoodlums?"

Deante turned to Christian as he was being hand-cuffed by another officer. "Go on, get outta here," he urged. "Get to stepping."

Show me your friends and I'll show you your fu-ture—that's what several folks had often told Christian. He understood that they were right. Still, he felt a certain kinship with Deante and felt bad about leaving him that day. Deante wouldn't have left him. And Christian wasn't quite convinced that the way Deante settled things was totally without merit.

D-man stood over the sink in the garage and washed grease off his hands. Christian tossed him a towel that hung nearby.

"So maybe we'll hang out and watch the games one Sunday," Deante suggested.

"Maybe," Christian said.

Chapter 37

Tobias parked in the overflow lot above Wallace Lake in Berea, out of sight of anyone parking in the main lot but close enough to observe people coming or going from the boat ramp. There were a few cars parked in the lot below, a lone fisherman sat on a bench near the edge of the water, and two boats were already on the lake. He switched on the small interior light above the dashboard, put in a CD and adjusted the volume, and then opened one of the photo albums Donna had given him.

In one photo, Elton tried to help Lakisha balance herself on a small bicycle. The seat had been adjusted as low as it could go, and the brackets that had once held training wheels in place were still attached. Probably her first bike, Tobias thought. It was red and silver and had colored panels between the spokes and a bell on the right side of the handlebars. Tobias tried to remember if he'd

ever had a bike that nice. But all he could recall were the
used bikes he bought from the junkyard or the Goodwill,
or the one he'd stolen once after the owner left it unat-
tended outside a supermarket on Central Avenue.

Elton appeared nervous and excited as he prepared to
let go of the bike. Tobias wondered who took the photo—
perhaps Sugar, or perhaps the girl's mother. He wondered
whether Lakisha was a quick study, wondered how many
attempts she'd made before she was able to take off on
her own, experience the freedom that comes with mobili-
ty.

In another photo, Elton lounged in shorts and a T-
shirt at what looked like a campground. Lakisha was in
the background playing with another little girl. Both held
long sticks with marshmallows on the ends. Elton had a
beard and neatly trimmed moustache. In the distance, behind them, there appeared to be a covered area where
people were gathered. Who were these people? Random
folks sharing a public space, or part of a group of friends
and family Elton had structured for Lakisha? Where were
these people now? Would he be able to create such a
support group for Lakisha in Cleveland?

He turned the page and saw Lakisha's face popping
out of a sea of colorful balls—perhaps at an amusement
park—Lakisha blowing out candles on a vanilla-frosted
birthday, and Lakisha posing in a dress outside a building.

She looked like a child and a young woman at the
same time. Her maturing body seemed inappropriate for
the dress she was wearing, but her smile suggested inno-

cence, an ignorance of the world that surrounded her. Who was left to protect her? Tobias felt a tremendous sense of inadequateness—probably the same feeling his mother must have felt raising him hundreds of miles away from her home and family without a husband. But there was no time for pity. He needed to suck it up and handle his business as his mother had.

In the lot closest to the lake, a pickup truck hauling a small boat behind it pulled in. An older man got out of the passenger side. He waited as the driver backed the boat down the ramp, and then he unhitched the boat from the carrier.

The driver pulled away from the ramp and parked. He joined the older man at the boat, and they headed out onto the lake. Tobias glanced at the clock in the car and noted the time Adrian Wilson and his son arrived. Wilson appeared thin and frail, and he moved sluggishly. The driver, whom Tobias assumed was Wilson's son, shared his father's stocky build and reddish-blond hair.

Tobias closed his eyes and took a deep breath. He knew what he had to do. When he opened his eyes, they were filled with tears. He got out of the SUV and opened its back hatch, removing a large shoebox and a shovel. He walked into the thick brush and started forcing the shovel into the ground. After digging a hole, he opened the box and examined its contents—two small caliber guns, a large hunting knife, and a pair of rusting brass knuckles. He'd given his shotgun away years earlier. He wiped his tears, closed the box, and placed it into the hole.

He took a deep breath.

"Bury it," he said. "Bury it."

Chapter 38

Pauline Davis's East Cleveland home was across the street from a boarded-up, mid-rise apartment building, in-between two abandoned houses. North of her home, separated from the interstate by a large privacy wall, were two occupied homes.

A narrow porch leading to the front door ran along one side of her home, and it was framed on the other side by a driveway in which a disabled car sat behind a pile of black, plastic garbage bags. A chubby, balding man rummaged through the bags. The wind blew off a blue tarp that covered a section of the home's roof, exposing a hole caused by rotting wood.

Tobias rattled the metal screen door with his fist. He knocked several times before he got any response.

"Who is it?" a voice finally called out.

"Looking for Pauline Davis," he announced.

A middle-aged woman made her way to the door and looked out.

"Pauline Davis?" Tobias asked.

"Ain't been Da—Dav—is for years," the woman slurred from the other side of the security door. "What can I do for ya?"

"Are you Kendall Davis's sister?"

"Kendall's dead," the woman blurted out, beginning to close the door. "Don't know anything 'bout her business."

"Ma'am, I'm here to talk to you 'bout her granddaughter," Tobias said. "Can I please come in?"

Pauline eased the door open a bit wider. "Who did you say you was?" she asked.

"Tobias Winslow."

She opened the screen door and invited him in. She pointed to a chair. He removed scattered newspapers off the chair and sat in it. She sat across from him on a couch. Next to him, a five-gallon bucket collected water dripping from the ceiling. The coffee table between the chair and the couch was littered with empty liquor bottles and beer cans. He smelled liquor on Pauline's breath.

"So, you're Sugar's sister?" Tobias asked.

She smiled. "Ain't heard that nickname in years," Pauline noted. "Yes, she was my sister."

"Pauline. Can I call you Pauline?"

"Why sure," she answered, smiling. "Get you something to drink?"

"No thanks. Were you two close?"

"Wouldn't say that," Pauline replied. "Kendall ain't had much to do with us after she left Cleveland. Saw her every once in a while. Last time—last time was at my mom's funeral."

"Did you know her son, Elton?"

"I knew *of* him. Saw photos. Ain't never met him in person."

"Well, Elton had a daughter," Tobias explained. "Sugar's granddaughter. My granddaughter."

She tilted her head and made eye contact with him. "You and Sugar was together?"

"No. Not really. Thing is, Lakisha—that's the granddaughter. She's coming to Cleveland, on account of her father, Elton, is dead."

"Mr. Winslow, I'm not seeing what any of this has to do with me."

"I'm thinking your family might want to be involved with Lakisha. Might want to connect with her since you are her family."

Pauline stood. "I'm sorry 'bout your son. But you can look around here and see I ain't able to tend to no child, not at my age. I don't have much money. Don't see how I can help."

"No, no," Tobias said. "I'm not looking for any *financial* help. Between the money from the government to take care of Lakisha and the money Elton had in the bank, Lakisha's good. No, I'm talking 'bout family support." He stood and placed a card on the coffee table. "This has my name, address, and phone number, Pauline," he said. "Please, think 'bout what I said."

"Sugar and I, we were never close," Pauline said. "But I don't recall ever hearing your name."

"That's 'cause we were never together," Tobias explained. "Just found out that Elton was my son. That Lakisha is my granddaughter."

Chapter 39

The students in the FDU amphitheater stood and clapped. Maddie slowly mouthed the words "Thank you," and Joey made her way across the stage to the podium.

"As promised," Joey said. "This has been a quite delightful evening with the most delightful of women." She turned to Maddie and bowed. "Thank you, Mrs. Dubois, for sharing your time and experiences. There's so much to learn from them. Do you have time for a question or two?" Joey asked.

"Certainly," Maddie said.

Joey waded into the audience of college women with a microphone. She held it in front of one of the students.

"Mrs. Dubois," the student stated. "You spoke about a sense of community pride when you were attending college. What did that look like?"

"That's a great question, young lady. What it looked

like was people in my hometown who had a personal
stake in my success," Maddie related. "One semester I
had what you would call a shortage of funds. Feel me?
Any of you ever had that problem?"

The students laughed.

"I worked summers to help pay my way. But one
summer, I didn't make enough to pay the bill," Maddie
explained. "Anyway, I didn't tell anyone other than my
mother. I guess she told others. One evening, there was a
knock at our door. It was one of the women from our
church, Mrs. Katherine Williams. She had collected money from people in the community to pay my outstanding
bill. I'll never forget what she said. 'You take care of
your business in the classroom, and we'll make sure the
bill gets paid.'"

Another student raised her hand. "Was anything expected in return for that money?"

"Yes," Maddie responded. "I was expected to go to
school and to do the best I could. Apply myself. Once I
got a degree, it was expected that I wherever I went, that I
would do everything I could to help other black folks
succeed. My success, you see, was also the community's
success. We were all in it together."

Joey walked back to the stage. "Since I have the mic,
I get the last question," she said. "Why do you think that
sense of community no longer exists?"

"The family," Maddie answered. "Once the family
breaks down, there's no one to instill it. No one to teach
that family history. You have to understand where you

come from to have any chance of getting where you want to go."

"Well said," Joey commented, turning to the audience. "Please, let's show Mrs. Dubois our appreciation one last time."

The students stood and clapped, and a small crowd of women gathered around Maddie. Offstage, Christian approached Joey.

Joey greeted him with a smile.

"Thank you for making the arrangements for your aunt to be here," Joey told him.

"You're welcome," he said.

She noticed a look on his face she'd not seen before. "What?" she asked.

"There's this really nice Cajun restaurant I think you would like," he said. "Perhaps we could go there sometime?"

She paused. "Like a date?"

"More like two people at the same place, at the same time, enjoying a meal," he clarified. "I guarantee you it's the best Cajun food you'll find in Ohio."

Truth was, she liked his family—Maddie, Daija, and Cordell—more than she liked him. It was the type of family structure she'd always envied. She also loved the idea that he loved his family. He didn't seem to be the type that would ever walk away from it. What harm would learning more about him do?

Chapter 40

*V*ernita walked toward the fence that separated the institution from the road. She stopped ten feet from the fence, fell down on her knees, and stretched her arms to the sky.

"Our kin, they must be together!" she chanted. "Our kin, they must be together. Willie's soul won't rest 'til it happens. The boy's soul needs to rest. Our kin, they must be together. Our kin, they must be together."

***

Chante shook Tobias until he woke. He wiped his eyes as he sat up on the cot in the stockroom.

"What are you still doing here?" she asked. "I was about to set the alarm before I saw the light on in here. If you set that alarm then someone sets it off, the police will come shooting first, asking questions later."

"You right about that," Tobias agreed. "Must've dozed off. Haven't slept in days."

She helped him up, and they walked into the main area of the barbershop.

"This has been a tough couple of weeks for you," she acknowledged. "Can't imagine any man finding out that he had a son and a granddaughter in that way. I can see why you're not sleeping."

"It's not just Lakisha keeping me up," Tobias confided. "I've been having terrible nightmares."

"Nightmares? About what?"

"Some crazy woman screaming 'bout her dead son," he answered. "Think it's got something to do with that damn Dreamer group I told you 'bout."

Chante grasped his hand. "Crazy woman? Dead son? You ought to see someone," she suggested.

"What would I tell them? That I'm having visions of some woman I've never met screaming 'bout her dead son? That's likely to get me put away," he hypothesized.

"You think maybe there's some meaning to the nightmares?" she asked.

"Meaning?"

"Yes, perhaps some dead relative trying to tell you something."

"Now you're sounding crazy." Tobias noticed Chante's matching outfit and smelled her perfume. "Going out with that Antonio?" he asked.

She smiled. "He's taking me to see a play at Karamu House," she answered.

He shook his head.

"I don't have a good feeling about him. You trust him?"

"I'm a grown woman," she pointed out. "I can handle myself. I think you need to focus on your granddaughter. And go see somebody about them nightmares."

"You're right. You're right," he agreed. "But I do worry 'bout you."

Next to Tobias, sitting on a wooden crate, was a small, open box, with a white prescription bag protruding out of it. Chante picked up the stapled, white bag and peeked into the box.

"What's this?"

He didn't answer.

"Is this the blood pressure monitor the doctor gave you?"

"Yes, I guess it is," he answered.

"Aren't you supposed to be checking your blood pressure every day?"

She looked at the date stamped on the receipt on the prescription bag and then opened it.

"It's against the law to go through other people's medical records without their permission," he said.

She tilted her head and glared at him. "This package hasn't been opened. You haven't taken any of this medication. Why'd you even go to the doctor?"

"'Cause I was sick. And I needed a test."

"It doesn't make any sense to visit the doctor, pay him, and then ignore his advice. Wouldn't it be easier not to go, keep doing what you're doing, or not doing, and keep your money in your pocket. At least then, whoever's going to get your money after you croak will have more of it."

Chapter 41

As he pulled into the parking lot, Tobias glanced at the address he'd scribbled down on a piece of paper: *Entrance C, Euclid Square Mall.* That was the address listed in the packet of materials he'd brought back from the event at the park—where the meeting of the Wilfred Foster Society was scheduled to be held. Was it a misprint? There was a decent amount of cars parked outside the designated entrance, but why would anyone be meeting at a vacant mall that had been dead for more than a decade?

Perhaps, it was fitting. Folks gathering at a dead mall to reminisce about a dead relative. The mall had once been a symbol of commercial success—large stores, restaurants, attractions for children. Now it sat practically empty off Interstate 90, with few tenants and even fewer ideas for a better use for the land. None of that mattered. Tobias had to find out what was causing the frightening visions he'd been having of Wilfred's mother and how he could stop them.

Dealing with the unexpected arrival of Lakisha was tough enough. With the right team of people by his side, it was possible he'd be able to do right by the girl. But there was no way he could deal with both Lakisha and visions of some unhinged woman in an insane asylum.

A sign inside the mall entrance had names of different tenants and arrows pointing in the direction of their rooms. Judging by the names on the sign—The Glory Temple of Praise, Joshua's House of Worship—most of the fifteen or so tenants were churches. He'd never spent much time at malls, he had no money to spend at them, but the idea of a church being at a mall or what once had been one appeared out of place, as his few visits to malls could not have been less about God or worship.

A separate sign pointed visitors to the room where the Dreamers were meeting. Inside, there were about ten round tables. Few people were at the tables as most huddled near a refreshment area getting drinks and hors d'oeuvres. An older woman who had been recognized as one of the leaders of the group during the park event— and whose picture and name were in the program—sat by herself at a table. Tobias nervously approached her.

"Madeline Dubois?" he asked, offering his hand.

"Yes," she answered.

"Tobias Winslow. We met briefly at Luke Easter Park. I brought my aunt, Bessie Mae Edwards."

Maddie smiled. "Bessie Mae. Bless her heart. Is she okay?"

Tobias sat down across from Maddie. "Oh yeah," he answered. "She's doing 'bout the same. She's in a place not too far from here. Can't get out much. I try to get over to see her as much as I can."

"Well, it was so good to see her at the park. It's important that we recognize folks who helped get us off the ground. Your aunt, when she could, did a lot of legwork for us. I consider her family. Of course, she is family, if she's part of this group. So are you."

Tobias forced a smile. He hadn't come to hear about some murder in Louisiana years ago. No, he preferred to leave Willie and Vernita in the past. He had more-important matters at hand. "I was hoping I could talk to you about something. About Louisiana," he stated.

"Well, okay, Tobias. Mind if I call you Tobias?"

"No, ma'am."

"I know more than most, at least when it comes to our folks and Louisiana. What is it you're looking to find out?"

"Visions," he said. "I'm having visions. Not good ones."

She gave him a perplexed look. "Visions?" she asked. "I'm not a psychologist."

"Of course not," he said. "But I think you might be able to tell me what they're about."

She took a sip from her coffee mug. "I'm not really understanding," she said.

"These visions," he explained. "I think they're about Wilfred Foster. The woman in the visions—I think she's his mother."

Maddie smiled. "You mean Vernita."

"You're smiling," he observed. "Believe me, there's nothing amusing 'bout these visions. They're downright frightening."

"Not amusement," she commented. "Fate."

"Huh?"

"Have you spoken to Bessie Mae about this?"

"Her mind's not really clear these days."

"When Willie disappeared, he was engaged to be married. I'm not sure what happened to his wife-to-be. But folks say that his mother, Vernita. They say whatever happened to Willie eventually drove her crazy. They say the visions won't end until one of Willie's descendant's is united with one of his fiancée's offspring."

Tobias looked across the room. Could all of these people—professional-looking folks with good jobs and educations—believe this mumble jumble? It sounded like some backwoods folklore. "What does this have to do with me? With these visions?"

"Perhaps, the two people who must get together are close to making it happen," Maddie offered. "Are you in a new relationship?"

"Who me?" he asked. "You think it could be me?"

"Must be a reason you're having these visions."

The only new person in his life was Lakisha. But even if she was the person destined to be united with someone else, she was years away from being joined with anyone in that way. None of this made any sense, so Tobias changed the subject. "Did you know Wilfred Foster?"

"I knew *of* him," Maddie declared. "Everybody in that part of Louisiana did. Never met his family until years later."

"Tell me 'bout him."

"Not really much I can tell you that you can't find in an internet search. You've researched it?"

He gave her a blank stare. "I understand that 'something' bad, very bad, happened to him," he offered.

"Well," she started. "He disappeared in sixty-four. Believe he was twenty-five at the time."

"Disappeared?"

"It was very common back then," she explained. "Black folks disappeared all the time. Sometimes, they'd be found hanging from a tree or in a barn. Other times, their bullet-riddled bodies would be found by the side of the road or the edge of the river."

"He was never found?"

"They found his car abandoned behind a bowling alley," she said. "Bloodstains in the car, a necktie tied in the shape of a noose hanging on the rearview mirror."

"What'd he do?" Tobias asked.

"It's anybody's guess," Maddie replied. "The list of things that could get you lynched, thrown in the river, or your home firebombed changed from day to day. Could've been something simple as looking at a white person the wrong way." She looked at her empty coffee mug. "Sure I can't get you something to drink?"

"No thanks."

"As I said, usually the bodies were found," she continued. "White folks wanted us all to see what happened when we stepped out of line. Because his body was never found, the case has kind of reached legendary status."

"Who do you think was responsible?"

She shook her head. "Some say the sheriff. Some say the Klan," she answered. "How long have you been having these visions?"

"Just started," Tobias confessed. "They come and go." He shook his head. "Shame what happened to that young man, Wilfred. Shame that no one ever paid for the crime. Somebody should have paid."

"Oh, we've all paid," Maddie commented. "Many of us had to flee our homes, sometimes with only the clothes on our backs. We were killed, robbed, raped, maimed. You name it. I'm not sure we've ever recovered as a people. Neither has the country that allowed it to be done to us. Ask me, we all could use a cleansing."

"What do you mean?"

"Look what we've become, Tobias," she said. "Violence begets violence. Once you perfect it, you turn it loose on your own people. We've perfected killing, or haven't you seen the news?"

Tobias stood to leave. "We've learned from the best."

Chapter 42

Marcel swept the area around his workstation. Cameron worked on a customer in his chair while another sat in Tobias's chair, waiting for him to return from the back of the shop. Another customer entered.

"Can I help you?" Marcel asked. He put the broom and dustpan away and summoned Christian into his chair. Christian sat down. Marcel draped an apron around him. "What can I do for 'ya?"

"Take it down a bit, shape it all around," Christian instructed.

"Sure thing. You from 'round here?"

"No. Glenville," Christian answered. "In the neighborhood visiting a friend."

"Well, I'm glad you stopped in."

As Marcel switched the blade on his clippers, an older gentleman toting a large cooler walked into the barber-shop.

"Ruben, my main man," Cameron said. "What you got today?"

"Some of 'em coconut pies you like. Lemon too," Ruben announced. "And some red velvet cake."

"I'll take one of the coconut," Cameron said.

"How 'bout you, Marcel?" Ruben asked.

"I'm good."

Tobias emerged from the back of the shop. He put shaving lather into a small cup, spread it with a small brush across his customer's face, and then placed a warm towel over the cream. "Got any of that banana pudding, Ruben?"

"Friday," Ruben advised.

"So why you in here today?"

Ruben smiled.

Tobias sharpened his straight-edged blade and re-moved the towel. He paused as he eased the blade toward the man's face, his hands noticeably shaking. He put the blade down and closed his eyes. *Not now, Vernita*, he thought. *Not now*. He glided the blade down the side of the man's face and then put it down and looked at Cameron. "My partner's going to finish you," he told his customer. "I'm having a little problem with my hands today. On the house."

"You coming down with Parkinson's?" the customer asked.

"Naw," Tobias replied. "More like a case of Vernita."

Chapter 43

Sebastian's Place sat on a corner. A round canopy hung over the door. Inside, photos of Dizzie Gillespie, Ella Fitzgerald, and other jazz greats graced the walls. Their music saturated the dining area. Red tablecloths covered square tables, and servers wore large white chef hats with images of lobsters on them.

Christian and Joey sat at a table facing a large window looking out onto the street, watching vehicles make their way past the restaurant.

"So what do you recommend?" she asked.

"I pretty much get the same thing every time," he said. "Fried scampi. Afraid I'm not very adventurous that way. But I have it on good authority that everything here is good."

"I have your word on that?"

"Indeed."

Sebastian emerged from the kitchen and walked over to their table. "To what do I owe this pleasure?" he asked, looking at Christian.

"A man's got to eat," Christian answered. "Sebastian, this is Joey."

"Please to meet you, Joey," Sebastian said.

She smiled and nodded. "My pleasure."

"Are you ready for some authentic Cajun cooking?" Sebastian asked.

"You have no idea," she replied. "This chicken remoulade sounds delicious."

"It is."

"Okay then," she said. "Chicken remoulade it is."

"Regular for you, Christian?" Sebastian asked.

"Yes, please."

Sebastian placed his hand on Joey's shoulder. "Make sure you leave some room for dessert," he suggested. "I've whipped up some pepper ice cream. Some other specials too."

"You're killing me," she said. "My stomach may burst before I get out of here."

Sebastian looked at the center of the table and noticed there were no dessert menus. "Princess," he called out. "Can you please bring out those dessert menus and put them on the tables, like I asked you?"

Daija peeked out from behind the kitchen door. Then she ran past Sebastian and hugged Joey.

"Princess, what in the world are you doing?" Sebastian asked.

Joey smiled.

"Am I missing something?" Sebastian asked.

"Daddy, this is Miss Joey," Daija explained. "The one I told you about from grandma's house."

He smiled. "You've made quite an impression on my children," he said. "They've been talking about this mysterious visitor Christian brought by grandma's house for weeks now."

"Oh, that's so nice." Joey stated. "You have a wonderful family."

"Thanks," he replied. "Princess, go get those dessert menus. I'll be back with your meals in a bit."

Joey studied the surrounding scene—the customers enjoying their meals, a few chatting alongside a small bar, the Louisiana feel punctuated by the blues music playing in the background.

"This brings back memories," she marveled.

"Thought you'd like it," Christian proclaimed. "And it will give us a chance to get better acquainted."

"I'd like that too," she said, smiling. "So Sebastian's married to your cousin, Kenzie?"

"Yes. She does the books. He handles the food and drinks. They're planning on opening a second spot on the west side."

Joey reached for his hand. "At first I thought it was a little weird when you took me to your aunt's house. I mean, who does that?" she asked. "But I'm so glad you did."

Sebastian reemerged carrying a large tray with appetizers on it. "Get ready to be wowed," he said.

Chapter 44

S cuse me. Can I have your 'tention, please?" A man stood in the entrance of the barbershop. His old Cleveland Indians baseball cap was tattered, his T-shirt was dirty and worn, and his pants were too large but were held tightly to his waist by a thin cord. "Don't mean to disturb you folks," the man continued. "If I had any other choice, I wouldn't be here. Yesterday, my house burned to the ground. You may've seen it on the news. Right off Kinsman, near Ninety-Third."

"Oh, yeah," one of the customers in the waiting area affirmed. "Think I heard something 'bout that."

Tobias ignored the man and kept working on the customer in his chair, Cameron looked up at the stranger with a determined frown, Marcel stopped what he was doing.

"Everybody's okay. Thank God for that. But right now, my family and me are homeless. I'm doing what I can to provide for my wife and my four children," he volunteered. "Anything you can give, I'd appreciate. Just trying to get back on my feet, especially for my children."

The man pulled an empty soup can from his jacket. He shook the can, rattling the change inside as he walked past customers in the waiting area. One customer put a dollar into the can.

"God bless," the man replied.

Another emptied his pocket of all his change and dropped it in the can.

"Appreciate it," the man said.

He walked toward Marcel, who reached into his pocket and gave the man ten dollars. Cameron methodically moved away from his workstation into the open area between the barbers. The man extended the can to Cameron, who swatted it out of the man's hand, knocking the change and cash onto the floor.

"I saw you two weeks ago outside the grocery store with the same sad story!" Cameron shouted. "You damned liar!"

Embarrassed, the man kneeled and quickly began putting the money back into the can. Cameron kicked the can out of the man's hand toward the door.

"You better take that sad lie someplace else!" Cameron commanded, hovering over him. "You trifling SOB."

Tobias moved between Cameron and the man, who picked up his can and rushed out the door. While the customers high-fived each other and laughed, Cameron picked up the ten dollars and handed it to Marcel. He threw the remaining coins in the man's direction.

"A little riled up today, huh?" Tobias asked.

"Gonna be a bad day," Cameron lamented. "Realized that when I read the paper. That ain't the worst of it."

Tobias didn't inquire further. He accepted payment from the customer, who got up from his chair, and waved the next one forward.

Cameron folded a section of the *Call & Post*, the weekly black newspaper, and placed it on the counter near Tobias's workstation. Tobias didn't ask Cameron about the paper. Instead, he worked on the customer in his chair.

Cameron waited until Tobias finished. "Might wanna take a look at that," he suggested.

Tobias reluctantly lifted the newspaper to his face and viewed a photo of a couple at some fancy gala. "What's this?" he asked.

"Read the caption," Cameron urged.

"Isn't this that fella chasing Chante?" Tobias asked. "Antonio whatever?"

"Yeah," Cameron confirmed. "Read the caption."

Tobias put on his reading glasses and read it aloud.

"Businessman Antonio Cochran and his wife, Annette." He stopped in mid-sentence. "Oh, no," he said. "No, he didn't."

"Think Chante knows?" Cameron asked.

"Don't know," Tobias sighed. "Don't care. Ain't none of my business."

"You not going to tell her?" Cameron asked.

Tobias stared at Cameron. "She's a grown woman.

I'm not going there. And if I were you, I'd stay out of it. You don't want to go there."

"Don't you think she needs to see that?"

"She does need to see it—if she doesn't already know," Tobias said. "Don't make me the messenger." He tossed the newspaper in the trash. Then, he made eye contact with Marcel and Cameron. "Stay out of it," he warned.

About forty-five minutes later, Chante walked through the door and headed straight into the beauty shop. She spent several minutes organizing things before her first customer arrived. Then she came back into the barbershop and poured herself a cup of coffee.

"Somebody gonna show her the newspaper?" Marcel asked.

Tobias looked at Cameron then over at Marcel and lifted a finger to his mouth. "Don't think she reads that one," he said. "She doesn't follow sports that much."

"No, she doesn't," Cameron said. "She wouldn't be interested."

"Didn't you say she needs to see it?" Marcel asked. "'Fore you threw it in the trash."

Chante stared at Marcel. She walked over to the trash and retrieved the discarded newspaper. She took the newspaper and went back into the beauty shop.

Tobias put his hands over his face. "Oh, no," he said. "Why'd you do that?"

Cameron glared at Marcel.

"You said she needed to see it, didn't you?" Marcel asked.

Less than a minute later, a loud scream followed by the sound of shattering glass reverberated throughout. Chante reemerged and headed straight for the door, carrying the newspaper.

"You okay?" Cameron asked.

She rushed past him without answering.

Chapter 45

Outside the administration building, FDU students enjoyed an unseasonably warm fall day. Several tossed Frisbees back and forth, others spread colorful blankets across the massive lawn, Christian and Joey sat on the building's steps.

"When you're around my Aunt Maddie and my cousins, does it remind you of being back home? In Louisiana?" he asked.

"Well, sort of," she answered. "They remind me of *part* of my family. Educated. Professional. Family-oriented. Always trying to do better for themselves."

"Most of your family like that?"

"Didn't say that," she answered. "Some are. Then there are some that always seem to be standing still, stuck in the same old, same old. Falling back on the same old, tired excuses."

"Yeah," he said. "I've got more than my share of

those relatives too. Never seem to learn all while the world is passing them by."

She shook her head. "Unfortunately, there's no medicine for a lack of common sense," she pointed out. She looked past the students on the lawn to the treetops in the distance. "Sometimes I do feel worlds away from home," she confided.

"What do you remember about Louisiana?" he asked. "Before you left?"

She smiled. "I remember that day I came home from school, right before the hurricane," she started. "My mom had our suitcases out, packing. I'm like 'Mom, where are we going?' She's like 'We got to go. TV says there's a huge hurricane coming. It's not safe to stay here.'"

"So all of your family packed and left?"

"No," she said. "Next day, we packed our car and headed out. Before we left, we went over to two of my relatives' houses to say goodbye and to make sure they were okay. They were sitting in their living rooms, smoking cigarettes, and drinking like nothing was about to happen. Mom's like 'Aren't you folks leaving? Aren't you afraid of the hurricane?'"

"They didn't leave?"

"No," she replied. "Got stuck in the floods and had to be rescued. No clean water or food for days. They were taken to the Superdome. Eventually, they were housed in government trailers in the north part of the state."

"But they all survived?"

"Oh, yeah. They survived. But every time I see them, they go on and on about how the government took too long to rescue them. 'What part of *leave* didn't you understand?'"

"Well, at least they survived," he interjected.

"As we were driving away along I-Ten, my mother said, 'You see, that's why some niggers' never going to succeed. They don't listen. Don't learn from their mistakes. Will find a way to blame other people for all their problems. God, I hope you don't have that stupid gene in you'"

"Sad," he opined. "Why do you want to go back there?"

"It's like your Aunt Maddie said at the women's meeting. We have a responsibility to help out our own."

"You got that."

"And there's one other thing…"

"What?"

She stared into his eyes. "Don't laugh," she requested.

"Okay."

"You promise?"

"Yes, go ahead."

"My family always said there's one special person for me. If that's true, he's probably there."

"Probably. But do you really want to find him? I mean, what if he's living in some shack in the woods, beer belly in place, chain smoking, and living off disability? Shooting possums for dinner?"

She rolled her eyes as she stood.

Chapter 46

Chante's Cleveland Heights apartment had two outside views. One overlooked Cain Park. When there weren't too many leaves on the trees, she could see the soccer fields in the distance. The other view was from a sliding glass door that led to the small balcony on the other side of her apartment. It looked out onto a convenience store, the top of a parking garage, and the busy thoroughfare heading north and south.

Although the soccer fields were empty this time of the year, Chante preferred to gaze at that tranquil landscape instead of the cars and people below her balcony. She was doing that when her doorbell rang. She hoped that Antonio hadn't somehow managed to get past the security door on the first floor. She was surprised when she spotted Tobias through the peephole. She opened the door, and he walked past her. He placed a white bag on the kitchen table.

"Did we have plans or something tonight?" she asked.

He didn't immediately answer. Instead, he headed to the large leather recliner in her living room. "Thought I'd better check and see how you were," he said. "That was quite a sucker punch you took."

"I'm fine," she said. "And I hope you don't make me regret giving you that spare key. What's in the bag?"

"Look and see."

She smiled when she opened the bag and smelled the barbeque.

"Figured if you going to sit in here stuffing your face and feeling sorry for yourself, you may as well have some good grub," he said. "And since you ain't much of a cook."

"This from Whitmores?"

"Of course. Got you a side of collard greens and some mac and cheese too. Still want that key back?"

"Why don't you keep it for a little while longer," she suggested. "And I *can* cook when I have the time. Come sit down and share this with me. I can't eat all of this."

She put the food on plates, tossed the plastic utensils that came with the order, retrieved her own from the kitchen, and then poured two glasses of water. He joined her at the table.

"Why do you think this *always* happens to me?" she asked.

"'Cause you got this thing 'bout plastic forks and knives," he joked. "Me, I use what they put in the bag. Then there's nothing to clean up afterward."

She glared at him. "That's not what I meant, old man," she corrected. "Why do I keep attracting these losers? Seem to be attracted to me like white on rice."

"Want to know what I think?"

"Not really. But you did bring dinner."

"Way I see it, when you grow up in the same area, see all the same folks all the time, you get to the point where you're too familiar with everybody in your circle. Then you start looking at folks outside your circle. It ain't that they any better. They're just new mysteries."

"What are you saying, Tobias?"

"The grass isn't always greener on the other side. Plenty of men walk into the shop everyday sweet on you. You ought to give one of *them* a chance."

"You think? Like who?"

"Well, there's Harvey."

"Harvey?"

He looked up from his plate. "That man ain't got but seven hairs left on his head. Do you really think he needs to stop by two, three times each week, always when you happen to be working?" He started mimicking Harvey. "Why don't you look *precious* today, Miss Chante. Mind if I ask what's that scent you're wearing?"

She laughed. "Leave that man alone. He can't help that he likes what he sees," she commented.

"Couldn't hurt to expand your playing field," he said. "They ain't all got fancy suits. Some don't talk so proper, but some are hard-working, respectable folks. Open your eyes." He smiled. "As much as I'd love to keep talking 'bout your love life, that's not why I'm here. Need to talk to you 'bout something else."

"What?"

He got up from the table and walked over to the window. In the distance, he saw a bicyclist entering the park and a couple walking hand-in-hand. "These social services people," he began. "They telling me I need to put together a team to help raise Lakisha. People I can trust, especially if something were to happen to me. And I have to appoint someone to look after her in case something *was* to happen to me." He pulled a paper out of his pocket, walked back to the table, and put it in front of her.

"What's this?" she asked.

"I'd like you to be part of that team," he said. "Like I said, I need to have someone who would be her guardian if something were to happen to me."

"Me?" she asked. "Didn't you tell me you went to visit her grandmother's people? Don't you think family would be better?"

"I don't think they're interested," he said.

"Why me?"

"You're smart. You're educated," he noted. "Lakisha could use a strong black woman. Teach her 'bout things only a black woman can teach another black woman. I don't know nothing 'bout raising no girl."

"You think I'm smart?"

"Yes," he concluded. "'Cept when it comes to men."

Reaching for the napkins at the edge of the table, Tobias accidentally knocked a sealed envelope to the floor. As he retrieved it, he noticed the word "VACATE" stamped across the envelope in red letters.

"You going on vacation," he asked.

She gave him a puzzled look before spotting the envelope in his hand. She snatched it away. "*Vacate*," she said. "Not *vacation*."

He tilted his head downward. "You ain't been paying your rent?"

"Of course I have been," she responded. "Not that it's any of your business. The building went condo last year. They're not going to renew my lease. I have ninety days to move."

"Whatcha gonna do?"

"Find a new place."

Chapter 47

When her front door opened, Maddie was sitting on the couch in her living room, examining a manuscript. Kenzie peered through the door. Cordell's head rested on her shoulders. Daija, barely awake, clung to her side.

"I'm going to put them down in back," Kenzie said softly.

Maddie smiled as she nodded. "Need any help?"

"No thanks. I'm good," Kenzie responded.

As Kenzie guided her half-asleep children to a bedroom, Maddie turned her attention back to the manuscript. She crossed out a large section with her pencil and then circled another passage that needed revision. She set the papers down on the coffee table and shook her head in frustration.

"What are you working on?" Kenzie asked, upon returning from the bedroom.

She knew the answer. About a year prior, her mother had written an article about Wilfred Foster for a national magazine. Since then, several folks had encouraged Maddie to expand the article into a book. Kenzie and others had convinced her that such a book could help them raise much-needed money for the foundation.

"What else?" Maddie commented. "The book."

Kenzie sat down next to her mother. "How's that going?"

"Afraid it's not going well. Wilfred Foster needs someone more talented than me to tell his story. I've been stuck in place for months."

Kenzie grasped her mother's hand. "There's no one better suited to tell Wilfred's story than you," she said, matter-of-factly.

"You think?"

"I know. What do you have so far?"

"Well," Maddie stated. "Much of it is stuff I already knew. Willie graduated from the Colored high school when he was nineteen. He lived with his grandmother and eleven siblings. They all worked in the fields. But he had no plans to work in the fields. He wanted to leave Louisiana and go north. He had cousins who had dropped out of school and went north."

"How was he able to avoid working in the fields?"

"Before he graduated high school, he had a friend whose father owned a juke joint."

"A what?"

"A black-run bar where folks drank, danced, gambled, and whatever else they could get away with. He would hang out with this friend of his at the bar, watching the illegal gambling in the back and all the other things that go on at places like that. He met a lot of folks there, blacks and whites. He learned various hustles. Then he lost his friend."

"What do you mean *lost* him?"

"They found his friend hanging from a tree. That scared Willie. Still, he wasn't ready to head for the fields. His mother said he had stars in his eyes. That he'd never be satisfied with the life society had mapped out for him. He got a job at a meat-packing plant outside of town. He also worked at two motels which were owned by someone he knew from the bar. But those were temporary. He told folks he was saving his money so he'd have something to live off when he went north—at least until he could find work."

"Why didn't he leave?"

"He was going to. Then he met a girl. Fell in love with her, and they got engaged. It took him a while before he could convince her that leaving was the best thing to do. Their entire support system was in Louisiana. She finally agreed that she'd leave after they got married. But that meant he had to save even more money for them to live off. Had to stay in Louisiana even longer. That was his undoing."

"What was he like? Personality wise?"

Maddie smiled. "He was a snappy dresser. In the few photos I've seen, he always wore a hat, often a tie. And apparently, he knew how to earn money. He saved enough to buy himself a fancy car. That was rare for a black man his age in Louisiana."

"Sounds like he was very industrious," Kenzie commented.

"And they say he had a way with words," Maddie continued. "Was comfortable around white folks. Maybe too comfortable."

"You think that's what got him killed?"

"Don't know."

Kenzie stood. "Sounds like you're off to a great start," she said.

"That's the problem," Maddie said. "Willie's life ended before it ever really got started. He was twenty-five years old when he disappeared. Can you imagine someone trying to write a book about the first twenty-five years of your life?"

Kenzie pondered the question. "That would be a challenge," she acknowledged.

"The tragedy here—and believe me there's many—is that we have no idea what would've become of Willie," Maddie said. "His potential was snatched away."

"Guess I never looked at it that way," Kenzie said.

"I've wrestled with that dilemma ever since I heard that boy's name years ago. And hundreds of other names for that matter. I'm not sure Willie would want to be remembered in terms of what happened *to* him. We can't continue to be defined in terms of what happened *to* us. It's too limiting."

Chapter 48

Seated on his couch, feet propped up on the coffee table, Tobias was watching football while enjoying a meal of smothered pork chops and mixed vegetables. He was talking to the television when the doorbell rang. He placed his plate on the coffee table next to the photo albums Donna had given him and lowered the television's volume.

"One second," he called out.

He made his way to the front door. When he opened it, he didn't immediately recognize the couple standing in front of him.

Pauline Davis was wearing a long dress with a flower pattern and a matching hat. The man he'd seen rummaging through the garbage in her driveway was now clean-shaven and sported a suit and tie.

"Can I help you?" Tobias asked.

"Hello, Tobias," Pauline said. "I'm Pauline. Sugar's sister. We met the other day, remember?"

"Oh, yeah," he said. "Didn't recognize you."

She looked over at the man beside her. "This here is Lester, my boyfriend."

"Nice to meet you, Lester," Tobias said. He opened his door and motioned them in. "Please come in."

Pauline and Lester sat in chairs opposite the couch.

"Can I get you something to drink, coffee?"

"No," Pauline answered. "We're good."

"I'm guessing you've thought about what we spoke about the other day," Tobias stated. "And I've got to tell you, I'd appreciate any help you folks can give me with this parenting thing. Frankly, it scares me to death."

"Well, sort of," Pauline responded. "That's what we're here to talk to you about."

Tobias turned off the television.

Pauline looked at Lester then hesitated.

"Go ahead," Lester urged. "Tell him why we're here, woman. We ain't got all day."

"We did a little checking for ourselves," Pauline advised. "Like you said, you and Kendall were never married. Best we can tell, you pretty much were a sperm donor."

"Wouldn't call it that," Tobias said. "But, yes, as I told you the other day, 'fore a couple weeks ago, I had no inkling 'bout Elton or Lakisha. Only met Kisha once."

Lester placed his hand on Pauline's thigh.

"What Pauline's trying to say is we ain't sure it's right that the government payments for the girl should go to you. As you say, we're her family—least Pauline is. Now, the boy's money, I can see that going to you. We ain't got no claim to that."

"What you trying to say?" Tobias asked.

"What we saying is, perhaps we can work out some deal concerning the girl's money and all," Pauline offered. "Don't make no sense to get lawyers involved and all of that. Do we really need to share a cut with them? There's probably enough money to make everyone happy. And with your business and the boy's money, what do you care?"

Tobias stood and walked to his door. As he did, images of the liquor bottles and beer cans strewn throughout Pauline's house flashed through his mind, as did her slurred speech and the bucket in her living room collecting water from the ceiling. He pulled twenty dollars out of his wallet as Pauline and Lester walked to the door. "This is how this is going to go," he instructed, taking a deep breath. "You two gonna take this money. You gonna go buy your whiskey or whatever. Drink it up. Smoke it up. That ain't my business. And we gonna pretend we never had this conversation."

"I have no idea what you're suggesting!" Pauline insisted. "And I certainly don't appreciate it! Our concern is that girl."

Tobias pulled an additional ten dollars out of his wallet. He then looked into Lester's eyes as he pushed the cash against his chest. "Probably won't be good if I see you or her again," he said. "Sometimes, I can be a bit impulsive. Hear what I'm saying?"

Lester clutched the money. "Let's get outta here, Pauline."

Chapter 49

At Kenzie and Sebastian's home near Elyria, a piano protruded from one corner of the spacious living room, next to a floor-to-ceiling fireplace, underneath the second-floor landing in the open loft. Maddie sat on the piano bench, her grandchildren on either side of her, teaching Daija how to play a simple tune.

"You ready?" Maddie asked her.

Daija nodded. Christian, Joey, and Kenzie, at the other end of the room, paused their card game and looked toward the piano. With one hand, Daija pressed the keys in rhythm and played "Mary Had a Little Lamb." They all stood and clapped when she finished. Daija smiled.

"Can you teach me?" Cordell asked, excited. "Can I do it too?"

"Of course," Maddie answered.

Daija and Cordell switched places. Kenzie, Christian, and Joey resumed their card game.

Sebastian emerged from the kitchen. "About fifteen minutes to show time," he announced.

Joey looked past the dining room into the large backyard. She noticed several wooden stakes near an oversized shed. "What are those stakes near the shed for?" she asked.

"The swimming pool," Christian answered. "And we don't call that a shed, at least not in earshot of Kenzie."

Joey glanced back into the yard and then glared at Christian with a perplexed look. "If it's not a shed, what is it then?" she inquired.

Christian looked at Kenzie, who was smiling. "You do the honors," he directed her.

Kenzie stood reluctantly. "Guess I'll have to now," she said, grasping Joey's hand. "Follow me."

They walked through the dining room and past the sliding glass door leading to the backyard, over the paved patio area to the shed. Kenzie entered a code on the electronic keypad and then opened the shed door. Inside, a small desk and easel sat in the middle of the shed. A wood-and-glass cabinet containing paintbrushes and supplies stood next to the desk. The walls of the shed were covered with paintings—family portraits, landscapes, various scenes from Kenzie's life.

"Wow," Joey commented. "Whose work is this?"

"They're mine." Kenzie said. "This is my studio, at least until the basement is finished and I can set up there."

"How long you've been painting?"

"All my life. It's my escape. My little piece of paradise. Not that I've had much escape time lately."

"This is much more than an escape. It's a calling. These should be displayed in a shop or an art gallery."

Kenzie smiled. "Thanks. You think?"

They left the shed and walked back into the house.

In the kitchen, Sebastian was placing capons on plates. "Hon, I'm almost done here," he advised Kenzie. "Why don't you see what everyone wants to drink, while I start making the gravy?"

"Sure," she replied.

"Homemade gravy," Joey noted. "Mind if I watch you work?"

Sebastian smiled. "Saddle up and watch a master chef work," he urged.

Kenzie went into the living room. Joey hovered near Sebastian.

He began melting butter in a saucepan. Then he stirred flour into the melted butter. He pointed to a bowl on the counter next to Joey. "Grab that broth please and pour it in," he instructed.

She lifted the broth and began tilting it toward the saucepan. He lifted his hand.

"Slowly mix it in," he guided.

"Okay."

He handed her a utensil. "Stir it slowly," he directed. "Slowly."

"For how long?"

"Until it thickens," he answered. "Then you're going to add the drippings and some seasoning. There you go."

She smiled as she stirred.

"How long have you and Christian been dating," he asked.

"We're not really dating," she responded. "That night at your restaurant was the first time we'd been out."

He stared at her. "You kidding? You two look like you've been dating for years. You've got the feel of an old, married couple."

⌾⌾⌾

Tobias carried a box of supplies and bottled water into the shop. He was setting it down near his work station when he heard a commotion coming from the beauty shop.

He approached the door separating the barbershop and beauty shop and eavesdropped.

"Don't want to hear anything you got to say," Chante shouted. "Already told you that. What don't you understand? And don't touch me! Take these flowers and get the hell out of here! Go give them to your wife."

"You're not going to let me explain?" Antonio asked.

"Explain what?"

"Like I told you, it's complicated. But it's not what it seems. Please give me a chance to explain. I'll make it right by you."

"Leave. Please leave," she demanded. "Don't come back again. And lose my number. Forget you ever met me."

"This really how you want it?" Antonio asked. "You

going to let a simple misunderstanding get in the way of business?"

"Misunderstanding? Business? Seriously?"

Tobias walked into the beauty shop. He faced Antonio. "Sir, I think you need to leave now," he suggested. "You ain't welcome here."

Antonio turned and faced Tobias. "This doesn't concern you, old man," he said. "You'd be wise to stay out of it. It's way, way above your comprehension level."

Cameron peeked inside. He made eye contact with Tobias and slowly lifted one hand up and down, as if to say, "Okay, Toby, think this through."

Tobias took a deep breath. "This is how this is gonna go," he stated, forcing a smile. "You either gonna walk outta here, or you gonna be carried out. Now think hard, young man. This is what you educated folks call a defining moment. Hope you can comprehend what a simple-minded old man is trying to tell you."

"What are you going to do if I don't?" Antonio asked, inching forward.

Chante stepped between the two. "He's not worth it, Tobias," she said.

Antonio picked up the flowers and began walking toward the door. He stopped in the barbershop and turned back to Tobias.

"I can buy and sell you," he declared. "You do realize that, don't you? Comprehend who you're messing with? With one phone call, I'll have every city inspector on the east side up in your business."

Tobias smiled. "Mister, you don't *know* me—and you really don't want to get to *know* me. But I'll tell you this. I'm not who I used to be. You wouldn't still be standing here if I were. But understand this, while I may not be that same person, I ain't forgotten everything. I remember enough to make this a very bad day for you."

Chapter 50

At the county social services office in downtown Cleveland, Tobias, Lakisha, Donna, and social worker Leonard Taylor sat in a large conference room. Lakisha fiddled with a toy while the other three mapped out a strategy. Leonard slid a manila folder across the table to Tobias.

"I'll be your contact person for everything," Leonard announced. "You have questions about anything, you call me, day or night. Anything. If I can't answer your question, I'll find someone who can."

"Okay," Tobias answered.

"You can call me at the office or on my cell," Leonard continued. "Lakisha will start school one week after she arrives in Cleveland. Her records have been transferred. There are a few forms in that file that you'll need to sign and return to the school, Mr. Winslow. I've also made copies for you to keep." Leonard looked at Lakisha.

"I suggest you and your grandfather visit the school before your first day. Meet the principal and some of your
teachers," Leonard advised. "It'd be a good idea to go
over the morning bus routine. Understand?"

"Yes," Tobias replied.

"Lakisha will have a special academic counselor at
the school. That person not only works with the school
district, but with our office. She's part of the team we've
assembled," Leonard pointed out. "We're going to do
everything in our power to support your family, Mr.
Winslow. It may also be a good idea to set up a place
where she can study while she's at the barbershop, especially if you're planning on the bus dropping her off there
after school—"

Donna looked up from the table. "Lakisha, at least
once a month you will meet with a therapist here in this
office," she said. "Those sessions will be similar to ones
we've had in LA."

"Are you coming to Cleveland?" Lakisha asked.

"Afraid not," Donna said. "Mr. Edwards will be doing the things I did. Like he said, he's put together a new
team for you. One right here in Cleveland."

"Why not?" Lakisha asked.

Donna reached across the table and grasped Lakisha's hand. "Because there's other young men and wom-
en in Los Angeles who need my help," she explained.
"But I've got you the best people in Cleveland. And
you've got my number."

"Tell me again 'bout the doctor," Tobias requested.

"Yes," Leonard answered. "Lakisha's primary care

doctor has an office in Shaker. That's a little closer to where you live. More convenient than having to come downtown. I'm still waiting to hear back from her office this morning, but I'd like you two to visit her before Lakisha flies back to LA. I believe she's gotten Lakisha's records from California. She'll do a physical and you'll be seeing her every six months or so—"

Donna smiled. "Mr. Winslow, do you and Lakisha have any special plans for today?" she asked. "Other than seeing the doctor?"

"Thought we'd go to the zoo," Tobias said. "Visit the barbershop."

"Sounds like fun," Donna said. "I'll pick her up tomorrow afternoon and take her to the airport."

A receptionist entered the conference room. She took Lakisha to another room while Leonard, Donna, and Tobias continued their discussion.

"Mr. Winslow, have you made any progress in terms of connecting with Sugar's family?" Donna asked. "Did you speak with her sister?"

"Well, 'bout that," Tobias started, pausing.

"Where you able to find her?"

"I'm thinking they're not gonna be involved," Tobias advised. "Think it's all a bit too much right now to wrap their heads 'round."

"Mr. Winslow, the larger the support system, the better," Donna stressed. "You've heard the saying—it takes a village to raise a child. I'd suggest you use every resource you can."

"Some villages ain't worth visiting," he commented.

"Nothing but ignorance and despair. Hear what I'm saying?"

"Well, perhaps that's something you can revisit another time, after Lakisha arrives for good. People have a way of coming around. And I think Lakisha could benefit from interaction with other family members, especially if there are some closer to her age. I don't want you to stop trying, okay?"

He didn't answer.

"There are two other things," Leonard interjected. "A part of the money you'll be receiving each month is designated for housing. Have you considered finding a different place? Perhaps one in a safer neighborhood?"

Confused, Tobias looked at Donna and then over at Leonard. "Something wrong with my place?"

"Well, there are *safer* places," Leonard commented. "And since the extra money wouldn't be an issue—"

"So I should be looking for another place?"

"Just saying."

Tobias exhaled. "You said two things…"

Leonard opened one of the manila folders in front of him. "I've been looking at your file, Mr. Winslow," he said. "Have you ever thought about an expungement?"

"A what?"

"It's the legal process by which the state can erase your criminal record," Leonard explained. "It's for people who were convicted of non-violent crimes who haven't re-offended. People who have turned their lives around. Looks like your case might be open and shut."

Tobias looked at Donna.

"I think he's right," she affirmed.

"What good would that do?" Tobias asked.

"It would say to the world that not only did you pay for your crime, but that you turned your life around. Became a productive member of society. Remove that one stain from your record," Leonard said.

Tobias stood. "I'm way past caring what other people think 'bout what I did to survive," he explained. "I always *wanted* to be make an honest contribution. Thing is, society had no interest in me."

❧❧❧

Cameron swept hair clippings, and Marcel and Chante were talking by the vending machine when Tobias and Lakisha walked into the barbershop. They stood in the waiting area as she looked in each direction.

"This your place?" Lakisha asked.

"Yes, this is where I work," Tobias answered.

Cameron put the small broom and dustpan down and approached. "Well, who do we have here?" he asked.

"Lakisha," Tobias said. "This is Mr. Maddox. He and I have worked together for the past fifteen years."

Cameron reached out his hand. "I've been looking forward to meeting you, Lakisha," he said. "Toby told us that his granddaughter was the prettiest girl he'd ever seen. But I thought it was just an old man telling stories."

She blushed. Marcel and Chante approached.

"This is Marcel," Tobias said, pointing over to one of the workstations. "He works over there."

"Hello, Lakisha," Marcel said.

She stared at his dreadlocks. "How long it take to grow those?" she asked.

"Two years," he said. "You like them?"

She smiled.

Chante reached out her hand.

"I'm Chante," she said. "I work next door."

"You cut hair?" Lakisha asked.

"Cut hair, shampoo hair, color hair, do extensions, you name it," Chante explained. "I do a little of everything. Would you like to come over and see my shop?"

Lakisha nodded yes, and then followed Chante into the beauty shop.

"The next time you're here, you could help me. Might be more interesting than hanging out here with the men," Chante proposed.

"That'd be fun," Lakisha said.

They disappeared into the beauty shop.

"So, you're gonna do this?" Cameron asked.

"Do what?" Tobias responded.

"Take in Lakisha? Move her to Cleveland?"

Tobias stood silent for a moment. "What choice do I have?" he asked. "I have a granddaughter from a son I never knew. I can either give her a place to stay and do the best I can, although Lord knows she deserves much better than me, or sit here knowing that hundreds of miles away my offspring is being shuffled from one bad situation to the another—not knowing whether she's dead or alive. What kind of person would do that?"

"Toby, I ain't saying it's not the right thing to do. What I'm asking is, are ready for this?"

Tobias took a deep breath and forced himself to smile. "Years ago, I came home one day and there wasn't much for my mother and me to eat. She was in-between jobs and money was tight. I think we had a loaf of bread and some applesauce. Maybe some milk. I ate some of what we had and then I got up and left."

"Where'd you go?"

"Found a friend a few blocks away. Followed him and he took me someplace where we could make some money. The next morning I came home with some canned beans, some fruit, and some luncheon meat. My mother never asked where I got that stuff from or how I got it. It really didn't matter. We had to eat, and I had to do whatever I needed to do to make that happen. It was understood."

"What does that have to do with Lakisha?" Cameron asked.

"I'm all she has—and she's all I have. And I must do whatever I have to do to make sure she's cared for. I didn't make any choice. It was made for me."

Chapter 51

*I*n a rather spacious room at the institution, six women either sat or stood silently, wrestling with their thoughts as daylight from a large picture window that dominated one of the room's walls flooded the area. An oriental rug covered a portion of the hardwood floor in the middle of the room, a small table holding a potted plant on a patterned tablecloth keeping it in place.

At the corners of the rug, four women sat in wood chairs. One's arms were crossed against her chest, two others stared out into the daylight past the window, and the fourth looked down as if praying, her hands intertwined. Another woman, draped in a long dress nearly reaching her ankles, stood against the table as if a statue.

Opposite the window, two women anchored themselves against the two-toned colored wall. One sat in a chair, silent. Vernita stood against the wall. She smiled as she repeated herself.

"You done good," she said, smiling widely. "You done good. Thank you."

꿔쩔

Lakisha gently shook Tobias's arm, awakening him from his daydream.

They were seated near the gift shop and concession area at the zoo, eating lunch. Tobias tried to recall the last time he'd been to a zoo, tried to remember any part of his childhood that wasn't about mere survival. He had a hard time understanding how a place as tranquil and serene as the zoo could exist in the middle of an urban jungle.

"Mr. Winslow?" Lakisha asked.

"Yes, hon," Tobias said.

"What should I call you?"

He pondered her question. "Call me whatever you want, hon," he answered. "Mr. Winslow. Grandpa. Tobias. Whatever makes you happy."

"My dad said you're not supposed to address adults by their first name," Lakisha informed him. "He said that's disrespectful."

"Well, he was right," he answered, nodding his head in agreement. "But it's not disrespectful if the person tells you it's all right. You and your father visit the zoo a lot?"

"Every once in a while. But I went with the school at least once a year. He liked the beach. And hiking. Any beaches around here?"

"All sorts of beaches," he revealed. "But most of the year, it's too cold to go into the water. But it's pretty to look at. Go out fishing for perch when it's warm."

A worker with a broom and a small dustpan made his way past the table where they were seated. Another zoo worker emptied a trash bin while a third sold T-shirts, trinkets, stuffed animals, posters, and toys. Tobias noticed Lakisha observing the zoo workers.

"I'm going to work at a zoo one day," she proclaimed.

He glanced at the laborers and then back at Lakisha. "I'm sure you can be whatever you put your mind to. Probably something real important like a doctor or lawyer," he suggested.

"I'm going to be a zoologist."

"A zoo what?"

"A zoologist. Someone who studies animals."

"Oh," he said. "That sounds like an important job."

"Is being a barber an important job?"

He paused as he considered her question. "I guess you can say it is. Folks have to get their hair cut. Especially those people who work the fancy jobs. Even the folks who don't, they like to look good for their partners. Did your father like animals?"

"Some of them," she said. "We had a lot of pets. Dogs. Cats. Gerbils. Tropical fish. He wasn't very good with the fish."

"Why do you say that?"

"We set up a tank. Then we went to the pet shop and bought some fish. One of the fish we bought was in a separate small bowl at the pet shop. Dad thought it was real pretty, so he bought it. Next day, he went back and got another fish that was in a separate bowl."

"And?"

"The fish in the separate bowls were separated because they couldn't live with the other fish without killing each other. But Dad didn't know that. He put them all in the same tank."

"Sort of like prison," Tobias commented. "Some folks need to be segregated, for everybody's sake."

"So the next day, we get up, and all the fish are dead except one."

"What happened?"

"One of the fish from the separate bowls killed all the rest," Lakisha said. "You have pets?"

"No," he said. "I have a hard enough time taking care of myself."

"Think I could have a pet?"

He grasped her hand. "Would that make you happy, hon?"

She smiled.

"We'll talk about it."

At the other end of the zoo, Christian and Joey sat on a bench at the duck pond. He looked beyond the water toward the tall buildings downtown in the distance. She tossed small kernels of corn to the geese and ducks gathered near the bench. The sunlight bearing down on them combatted some of the day's chill.

"What area of law are you considering?" he asked.

She smiled. "That seems like such a long way away," she responded. "First, I need to get into law school, get it paid for, get through it, and then pass the bar. What area do you think I'd be suited for?"

He hesitated. "Could definitely see you sending folks to prison," he stated. "You have a sort of unbending way about you. Don't think I'd want to go up against you in a courtroom."

She playfully slapped his hand.

"I seem harsh to you?"

He looked at the hair that peered out from under her hat, and then at her neck and shoulders. "No, not in every way," he teased. "Some things about you seem very gentle, warm. Worth exploring."

She blushed. "I'd ask what you mean by that," she retorted. "But perhaps I'll leave that alone."

"Your choice."

"Was it those gentle, worth-exploring things that prompted you to help me when I was stuck on the side of the road, or your desire to be a gentleman?"

"Both," he acknowledged.

"Huh?"

"I would've stopped even if you weren't easy on the eyes."

"I'm easy on the eyes?"

He didn't directly respond to her question. "What type of person would leave a colleague stranded? And yeah, you are. Easy on the eyes. Blind man could see that."

He took some of the kernels from her bag and tossed them into the lake. The ducks and geese turned from the bench and scrambled into the water.

"Ever hear of the Innocence Project?" she asked.

"Those the folks who work to free people from prison?"

"Yes," she answered. "I'd love to work for someone like that. Working to make sure the system works for everyone. Can't imagine how exciting that would be."

He pulled his head back and contorted his face. "Who are you?" he asked.

"Wouldn't you like to know?" she said, smiling. "What about you? What do you see yourself doing after graduation?"

"Think I'd like to get involved with community organizing. At least for a while."

"What do you mean?"

"Last summer, I worked with a group that organized people in distressed areas of Cleveland. Hough. St. Clair. Voter registration. Tenant groups. Lead abatement programs. There's so much work to be done."

"Sounds interesting."

"I loved it," he confessed. "Felt like I was really helping people. Sometimes, it seems like there's assistance available to help folks. But they have to have the right information."

"Thought about working with children?"

"No. Why?"

"I've watched you at the rec center," she admitted. "You're very good with children. They seem to listen to you. Respect you. That's something I've never had. A way with children, that is."

"You kidding, right?" he asked. "My cousins love

you. Last time I was there, I walked into the house and they're like, 'Where's Miss Joey?' No hello. No how are you doing? Nothing. Big letdown when they realized I was alone."

She laughed. "Actually, I really needed them."

"Why?"

"After the rec center, it's good to see children—black children—who seem to be living normal lives doing normal-kid things. That rec center can be so depressing."

He smiled. "Do you spend time with me because of me—or my adorable cousins?" he asked.

"Both," she said.

Chapter 52

Tobias glanced at the flyer he'd removed from the bulletin board in the barbershop—the one Sebastian had posted weeks earlier—and then at the address displayed on the mailbox at the end of the home's driveway and painted on the street-side curb. Yes, this was it—the place advertised on the paper. On the flyer, the home was photographed from a side angle. Still, the distinctive trees on the front lawn convinced Tobias he was at the right place.

As he walked to the front door, he noticed the home's slate roof, and wondered if maintaining it would be more expensive than maintaining a regular one. He also noticed the low-hanging gutters, which would be easy to reach with a ladder to clear leaves and debris. He could do it himself and not have to pay someone else.

He wasn't sold on the idea of moving. He'd lived in his apartment for nearly a decade. And while the area had begun to decline, his block had remained relatively stable, and he knew most of his neighbors. Not that he engaged with them much. Rather, since all the homes on the block other than the one he lived in were owner-occupied, it was easy to tell who belonged and who didn't. That provided a certain sense of security, even if many of the streets in the Lee-Miles area were waging an uphill battle against poverty, foreclosures, and crime.

His block was the ultimate contrast—a cobblestone street that spoke of a long-ago prominence and black, iron security bars affixed to most doors and first-floor windows. And since the upstairs apartment in the two-family home he rented was not far from the barbershop, he could return home to do errands during slow periods at work.

An agent pulled into the driveway before Tobias reached the front door. The agent scrambled out of his car and headed to the lockbox hanging from door knob.

"Good morning," he said, extending his hand. "You must be Mr. Winslow. I'm Ed Bacha."

"Good morning, Mr. Bacha," Tobias responded.

The agent fiddled with the lockbox until it opened and removed the key.

"That's slate, right?" Tobias asked, looking upward.

"Yes," Bacha said. "Nice touch, don't you think?"

"It is nice," Tobias responded. "Wondering if it costs much to maintain."

Bacha looked up as he opened the door. "I believe it may be cheaper," he said. "Usually, you have someone come out and inspect it every year, and they replace any bad pieces. I can certainly ask the homeowner about that."

Beyond the front door was a rectangular foyer. On the left side of the foyer was a staircase leading to the second floor and a study, which had a large window looking out onto the front yard and driveway and a floor-to-ceiling, built-in book case across an entire wall. Tobias didn't have many books. The few he had wouldn't fill half of one of the shelves. But this might be a good room for Lakisha. She could keep her school supplies and books here. And he could set up a desk and a computer for her here.

Straight past the foyer was the dining room. It had a sliding-glass door leading to a paved landing and the backyard. The living room was to the right of the foyer. Tobias walked through the dining room, stopped at the glass door, and peered out into the yard. He couldn't see much of the landscape, as it was covered with leaves, but he fixated on the tattered, above-the-ground, circular swimming pool.

"Not much use for an unheated pool in this part of the country," Bacha commented. "I'm sure the owner would be willing to take it down and get rid of it prior to transfer—at his expense, of course."

Tobias continued to stare forward. He recalled the DVD he watched on which Lakisha had molded a make-believe pool out of blue play dough.

"No," he answered. "I'd definitely want the pool to stay."

He glanced into the kitchen—new appliances, a wine

rack, an island in the middle of the room, and hooks above the island on which to hang pots and pans. He wasn't much of a cook, but it would be nice to have space to do it. Lakisha or someone else might use it.

The living room was immaculate—wood-burning fireplace, hardwood floors, and a skylight.

"What do you think?" Bacha asked.

"Very nice, sir," Tobias answered. "Very nice."

"I want to show you one more thing down here before we head upstairs."

Tobias followed Bacha back into the foyer and to a door that he assumed led to the garage. Past the door was a flight of steps.

"Where does this go to?" Tobias asked.

"It leads to an addition that was added on top of the garage," Bacha answered. "It's sort of a mother-in-law-suite with its own bathroom. You could rent it out to off-set some of your mortgage. It needs some finishing touches, but the space is great. Wish I had something like this when I was in college."

"Interesting," Tobias said.

Chapter 53

The home inspector Tobias hired sat in a folding chair in the foyer, checking boxes on his clipboard and jotting down the notes needed to complete his report. He'd already told Tobias that he hadn't found any problems that should rule out extending an offer on the home.

The landscaping in the backyard could be improved, to make sure water in one small area ran away from the home instead of toward it, and a tree overhanging the home needed to be trimmed, but otherwise both the home and property were in excellent shape. His complete report would come in the mail in a few days.

Chante and Tobias stood in the mother-in-law suite.

"What do you think?" he asked.

"Very nice," Chante commented. "You're moving up in the world. This would make a great home for you and Lakisha."

"No, no," he said. "What do you think about *this* space? The mother-in-law suite?"

She looked at him strangely. "Like I already said, it's nice. Could use a feminine touch here and there. But you could definitely rent it out and do okay. You could post an ad at Tri-C."

"I had another idea," he said. "I was thinking this might be a great place for you."

"For me?"

"You did say that you have to find another place."

"What? You and me live together—because I don't see enough of you at work?" she asked, jokingly.

"Not live together," he explained. "You'd be up here, in your own private space. Lakisha and I would be in the other parts of the house. Lord knows, I could use your help with her. I don't know anything about raising a child, let alone a girl. I'm worried I won't understand what to do—once the social workers and everyone else leave, and it's me and her."

"This is your solution? That's why you brought me here?" Chante asked.

He didn't answer. She wondered what other unsaid things were racing through his mind. While it would be nice to not live alone—some nights she dreaded returning home to an empty apartment—he'd have to be clear that this would be nothing more than an arrangement. She viewed him as an older-brother type. She enjoyed his company, cherished his fatherly advice, but would never see him in any other way. And while she could certainly help him with Lakisha, she was not ready or willing to be anyone's mother.

He had no designs on her either. But he wasn't prepared to raise Lakisha on his own. A boy would've been simpler. He'd be able to figure out what the boy was thinking. There was no way he'd understand what Lakisha was thinking or what she needed.

"Wow," Chante exclaimed. "I'm not sure what to say. You're right. I do need to find a place. But I'm not sure how this would work. You, me, and Lakisha."

"I'm not sure either," he responded. "But I like the sound of you, me, and Lakisha better than Lakisha and me. And something about this feels right. Believe me, there's not a lot that's been feeling right lately. We could try it for a while, see if it works? No harm, no foul."

She nodded her head as she glanced around the suite. "Give me some time to think about it," she said.

Chapter 54

As he approached the barbershop, Tobias noticed a young black man sitting in a parked car down the block in the driveway of an abandoned home. The young man made eye contact with Tobias and then quickly looked away, pulling a cap down over his eyes as he did.

Marcel was sweeping the sidewalk when Tobias reached the door. "Morning, Mr. Winslow."

"Morning," Tobias replied. "Is it Tuesday?"

"Naw," Marcel said. "Thought I'd do it, anyway."

Tobias took one step into the shop and then stepped back outside. "I've been thinking 'bout that idea you had 'bout the stockroom," he said.

"Huh?" Marcel said.

"'Bout you using it for a reading group or poetry readings."

"Oh, yeah?" Marcel recalled. "Yeah. A poetry slam! What you thinking?"

"Thinking it might work," Tobias admitted. "You could start out slow—a small gathering once a month. No more than fifteen people after closing one night…so long as you're careful 'bout who you invite. 'Course they'd need to come in through the side entrance, and the door to the shop would have to be locked—to make sure no one's wandering 'round where they shouldn't be or getting into things they shouldn't."

"That'll work," Marcel gushed. "I'm glad you like the idea."

"To be honest, I'm also thinking it'll be good to have that area cleared out," Tobias continued. "Might be a good place for Lakisha to do her homework when she's here. You clearing it out would be a big help to me."

"Ain't nothing wrong with that," Marcel responded. "I help you. You help me. I'll start taking them supplies down to the basement and cleaning out that space this weekend. Trust me, you'll be happy you did this. Lakisha can do her thing, and I can do my thing. It's all good."

About a mile away from the barbershop, Kenzie sent one text messages after another while Sebastian drove to the restaurant—one to Maddie to provide her an ETA to pick up the children, another to the contractor she was scheduled to meet later, others responding to text inquiries. When she looked up from her telephone, she noticed Sebastian wasn't taking the most-direct route to the restaurant.

"Babe, where are you going?" she asked.

"Need to make a quick stop," he answered.

"You do realize I've got to get the kids from Mom's?"

"You can be a little late this one time. I sure Maddie won't mind," he assured her. "And this is important."

"What is?"

"Remember that guy I told you I met at the barbershop a couple of weeks back? The Dreamer?"

"Yeah?"

"He put in a bid on our house. Wanted to say a quick hello. You going to love this guy."

Kenzie didn't love Sebastian's timing, but she couldn't fault his intentions. After all, she'd been the one urging Dreamers to take the time to get acquainted with other Dreamers and, thus far, she'd done very little of that.

"Okay," she said. "Five minutes. Then we have to go."

Sebastian cased into a parking space outside the barbershop. He and Kenzie exited the car and walked into the shop. The young man down the block from the shop looked up, spotted Kenzie and Sebastian entering the shop, and then looked away.

Moments later, however, he perked up when Deante came strolling around the corner and approached the shop. The young man braced himself as he waited for an RTA bus to pass.

"Dee," Cameron said, greeting Deante as he entered. "Dee—that time of the week already?"

"Always that time of the week," Deante replied. "But I'm here to get a cut and a shave. Been a good couple of weeks."

D-man sat in Marcel's chair. Cameron wiped down his chair with disinfectant. Tobias, Sebastian, and Kenzie stood around his station and chatting, joking, and laughing. Outside the shop, the young man got out of his car. He left the ignition running, tucked a weapon into his waistband, covered it with his hoodie, and then pulled a ski mask over his face. He looked in all directions, waiting until the block was relatively clear, and then rapidly moved to the front of the shop.

Reaching the front, the young man spotted Deante in Marcel's chair and pulled out his weapon. He sprayed automatic gunfire into the barbershop, shattering the plate-glass window on one side of the front entrance. Then, he tucked the weapon in his waistband, ran back to his car, and sped off.

Inside the shop, Cameron took cover behind his chair as Marcel held one of his legs, screaming in pain. Deante lay on the floor, applying pressure in an attempt to stop the blood gushing from his chest.

"Call nine-one-one!" he screamed. "Someone call nine-one-one!"

Kenzie and Sebastian both lay motionless; Tobias hung partially over his chair. Chante came running out of the beauty shop, screaming.

Chapter 55

In a private waiting area at the Cleveland Clinic, Maddie stood in a corner. Daija and Cordell slept in a chair. Christian sat in another chair, staring straight ahead, struggling to contain his anger. Joey walked into the room and embraced Maddie.

"I'm so sorry," she sobbed, tears streaming down her face. "I'm so sorry. I came as soon as I heard. How they doing?"

"Sebastian's gone," Maddie said. "They're operating on Kenzie now. All we can do is pray. Please pray for my daughter."

"I have been," Joey reassured her. "That's all I've been able to do since I heard." She walked over to Christian, sat on the arm of the chair in which he was seated, and placed her arms around him. "I'm so sorry," she whispered, clutching his hand as his tears flowed. "I'm so sorry."

He closed his eyes.

A doctor walked into the room. "Mrs. Dubois, I'm Dr. Chandral."

"How's my daughter?" Maddie asked.

"For now, she's out of the woods," Dr. Chandral informed her. "We've removed the bullets from her body. She's on oxygen because she's struggling to breathe on her own right now. We're hoping that will change in the next day or so. We're going to keep her in the emergency room for now."

"Thank you, Doctor," Maddie said. "God bless you."

Daija and Cordell opened their eyes. They slowly got up from their chairs, walked over to Joey, climbed into her lap, and then dosed back off.

☙❧

When Tobias regained consciousness, he was strapped to a bed in the emergency room at MetroHealth Hospital, an oxygen mask covering his nose and mouth, intravenous fluids flowing into two spots on one arm, and a blood pressure device strapped onto his other arm.

A surgeon removed the oxygen mask. "Hello, Mr. Winslow," the surgeon said. "I'm Dr. Taylor. You're one lucky man."

"How you figure?" Tobias managed to utter.

The surgeon dropped a bullet fragment on the tray next to Tobias' bed. "These bullets probably saved your life," the doctor commented. "I kept one of them for you as a souvenir."

"Bullets don't save lives," Tobias responded.

"You're right," Dr. Taylor agreed. "But with the blockage in your arteries, you were literally a dead man walking. Only a matter of time before you had a fatal stroke or heart attack. So getting you in here to remove the bullets allowed us to identify and begin addressing that problem." Dr. Taylor glanced at Tobias's medical chart. "And then there's the matter of your out-of-control, type-two diabetes. How long have you been a diabetic?"

"Didn't realize I was," Tobias confessed. He glanced around at his surroundings—the blue curtains on either side of his bed, the hospital employees working furiously at stations in the middle of the room beyond his small area. "How long have I been here?"

"Three days," Dr. Taylor answered. "After we removed the bullets, we had to place stents in your body and clear some of the plaque."

"Stents?"

"Small devices that'll help keep the blood flowing throughout your body."

"How long am I gonna be in here, Doc?"

"Depends. I'd guess two weeks. We'll be transferring you to a regular room probably tomorrow. After we get your blood glucose at acceptable levels, and after your doctor is sure you understand your medicine regime, you'll probably have to go to rehab for a few days. Probably going to take a while before you're walking normally."

"What day is it?" Tobias asked.

"Monday."

"Doc, I got to be outta here before two weeks."

"What? Do you have a hot date?"

"You could say that," Tobias said, smiling. "My granddaughter's coming from California to live with me. She's going to be a zoologist."

"That so?" the doctor said. "I'm thinking you might want to reschedule that visit, or at least postpone it, Mr. Winslow. Let's focus on you getting stronger. There's some people outside who've been waiting to see you. I've approved a short visit. But then you'll have to get back to resting. Okay?"

"Thank you, Doc."

After the surgeon left, Chante, Cameron, and Marcel entered the room. One of Marcel's legs was bandaged, and he walked with crutches. Cameron had a small bandage on his face where he'd been struck by shattered glass. The trio huddled around Tobias's bed.

Chante placed her hand over Tobias's. "Didn't know if we'd ever see you on this side again," she said.

"It'll take more than a couple of bullets to take me out," Tobias bragged. "How's everybody else?"

"I took some steel in my legs, but I'll be okay," Marcel said. "D-man just got out of the hospital. They say the bullets just missed his heart—"

Cameron interrupted. "Your friend, the Dreamer, he didn't make it," he announced. "And his wife's not doing so well."

"Who did this?" Tobias asked.

"Nobody's certain," Cameron said. "Deante was clearly the target, so it could've been anyone."

Chante eyed the bullet fragment on the tray. "We want you to know that we're here for you," she said. "And everything will be fine at the shop 'til you get back. You rest, hear me?"

"I'll try," Tobias said. "Hard to sleep with all these gadgets attached to me. And people poking and prodding every hour or so." He looked at Cameron. "Need you to do something for me, Cam."

"What's that?" Cameron asked.

"Go by my place and get me a change of clothes. Can you do that for me?"

"Sure thing."

Chapter 56

Does Mr. Wood have a record?"

In a second-floor room at Cleveland's City Hall, Mayor Emmanuel Wilkins stood between the city's police chief and an FBI representative. On a large screen to their right, a series of photos of Jamario Wood, the nineteen-year-old suspect named in the barbershop shooting, appeared on a screen. Several of the photos were taken from Wood's social media site and, in at least one, he was smiling and flashing gang signs with one hand and holding a wad of cash in the other. Posing without a shirt, it was hard to determine where one of Wood's tattoos ended and the next began.

As was his custom, Mayor Wilkins repeated the reporter's question and pondered it for what seemed like an extended period before finally answering. "I think that's a question that would be more approximately addressed to the county prosecutor," the mayor answered.

Wilkins's response didn't placate the reporter who seemed intent on letting everyone else in the room appreciate what he'd learned. "Our information is that this is the same person who, at seventeen, was arrested in the robbery and savage beating of a seventy-seven-year-old woman outside a supermarket in South Euclid. In that case, the elderly woman was beaten about her head with a rock."

The mayor forced a smile. "Do you have a question—or a statement you'd like to make?"

Some of the others in the room laughed as the mayor pointed to the next reporter. A woman with a matching hat and dress, standing next to a cameraperson, spoke into a microphone. "Mayor Wilkins, this morning there was a story in the *New York Times* about this shooting, and several other national media outlets are reporting the story. Are you concerned that the recovery that the city is touting across the country will be damaged by this sort of high-profile crime?"

"No," Wilkins answered quickly. "I'm not."

"Won't crime or the fear of it keep visitors away?"

"The last time I checked, there was significantly more crime in Chicago, New York, and Los Angeles. Yet none of those places seem to have a problem with attracting tourists," Wilkins said. "The average person who lives here, works here, visits here, faces no danger."

A group of hands went back up in the air. The mayor acknowledged another reporter.

"Mayor, you seem to be discounting the crime that has gripped many of the city's neighborhoods, especially on the east side, in the predominately black wards. Or is it that you draw a distinction between crime in the neighborhoods and crime downtown near the casino and sporting venues?"

The mayor struggled to prevent the expression on his face from displaying his growing anger with the line of questioning. "I'm not discounting crime that happens anywhere," he insisted. "As I said when we started this session, my prayers go out to all the victims of the barbershop shooting, and we're determined to bring to justice the one or ones responsible. We are also assisting the families."

Another reporter shouted a question before being called upon. "Mayor, what do you think is driving the crime on the eastside, in the black wards?"

Wilkins lifted his folded hands to his mouth as he considered the question. He carefully chose his words. There were times when he seemed to enjoy hearing himself speak. This wasn't one of them.

"People a lot smarter than me have been searching for that answer. I can tell you that we cannot police our way out of this problem—although the communities that you reference must work with the police to help us help them. We don't always get the cooperation and support that we seek. I realize there are historical reasons for that. I also think the breakdown of families has brought us to where we are today.

"Too many children growing up without fathers involved. Too many people who feel a sense of hopelessness. Too many people not taking advantage of the educational opportunities afforded them. None of that is going to be solved by politicians."

"What's the solution?" someone shouted.

"Wish I knew," Wilkins said.

രൗരൗ

A crowd began congregating outside the barbershop around eight p.m.—community activists, politicians, plus area residents drawn by the presence of several television crews. Below the shop's boarded-up, front window, a makeshift memorial of flowers, stuffed animals, empty liquor bottles, and sympathy cards rested on the sidewalk. Across the street from the shop in a vacant lot, Christian watched. He stared straight ahead, organizing his thoughts, as police circled the crowd. His cell phone vibrated. He glanced at it and saw it was Joey calling again and routed the call into voicemail. She had urged him to talk about whatever he was feeling, not to hold it in. He really didn't know what he was feeling, other than anger, and wasn't ready to talk to anyone.

An activist he'd seen on television lifted a bullhorn. "Yet again, we come together at the scene of a crime. At a place where at least one life was lost and others will be lost to the criminal justice system," the activist said. "We must ask ourselves, how long will we tolerate this? How long will we stand silent during this genocide?"

Someone in the crowd distributed small, white candles. As the candles were lit, photojournalists sprang into action. They trained their cameras on those holding the lit candles as they listened.

"If you've come here to make sense of senseless crime, then I urge you to go home," the activist continued. "We will never find answers that will make any of this right. Make any of this moral. Make any of this add up. But while we cannot explain the illogical, we can and must examine the conditions that have made our communities ripe for these tragedies. How long will our politicians play dumb while our communities are flooded with guns? How long will they resist common-sense restrictions that would keep guns out of the hands of criminals? Is the gun lobby more important than our children?"

A few folks clapped. Christian grew angry. *Criminals don't obey laws. How would more gun laws stop people who don't abide by those already in place? Have laws ever protected black people from rapes, lynching, or being burned out of their homes?*

The people who *needed* guns were those forced to live in these crime-infested neighborhoods.

The activist handed the bullhorn to the ward's councilwoman. "First, let me say that my prayers go out to the families of those injured or killed here," the councilwoman stated. "Please know that we will do everything we can to assist these victims. I'd like to speak briefly about the gangs that are controlling *some* of our streets. I say *some* because we know that this wouldn't be tolerated in *some* areas of our city. I urge all of you in joining me in calling for a return of community policing."

She looked toward the officers on the crowd's perimeter. "It does us no good for police to show up after these crimes have been committed. We need you to get out of your patrol cars, walk up and down these neighborhood streets, and get to know the people you are paid to serve and protect! What a novel concept. And someone should tell the mayor and the police chief that it would help if more of the officers looked like the people they serve. This may come as a surprise to the police union, but most of the people in this city are black. Is there are reason that most of the officers are not? We don't need officers who drive in from Parma, Mentor, and Strongsville, view us with contempt, and then race home to their all-white neighborhoods after their shifts end. Why can't we hire folks who live in Cleveland?"

Was it possible for police to be every place they needed to be? Why were people blaming the police instead of the people committing the crimes? Christian had no love for the police, but he had no misconceptions about who was responsible for this crime.

The crowd cheered as the councilwoman handed the bullhorn to a pastor.

He bowed his head and spoke softly. "Lord, have mercy on us sinners," he prayed. "Provide solutions to these problems we face. We lift these candles to you. They represent people who are willing to be used by you to solve this problem. Please provide us with the resources we need and the guidance we seek. In your Son's name we pray. Amen."

The pastor handed the bullhorn to the next speaker. Christian started his ignition. He'd heard enough. The only solution needed was eliminating the scoundrel who'd decided to settle his dispute by spraying gunfire into the barbershop.

Chapter 57

"iss Joey! Miss Joey!"

"Huh?"

A young girl tugged at Joey's sleeve, and that snapped her out of her daydream. She looked up from the homework papers she'd been grading, and smiled at Marquessa and Annette, who were standing next to her in the tutoring room at the recreation center.

"Can I help you?"

"How'd I do?" Marquessa demanded. "Did I get them all right?"

Joey shuffled through the pile of papers on the desk. She lifted her thumb as she handed Marquessa's assignment back to her.

"You got all the answers right," she informed her. "I'm so proud of you. And you should be proud of yourself. You don't need me to tell you that you can do this. Never forget that you can do this. And there's nothing wrong with asking for help when you need it. We all need help at times." She pointed to her head. "It's all up there." She glanced at Annette and then back at the homework pile. "Don't think I've graded yours yet," she advised. "I'm sorry."

Annette shook her head. "That's not what I want, Miss Joey," she said. "Mrs. Scott wants to see you in her office."

"Okay," Joey responded. "Thanks."

She walked to Mrs. Scott's office and stood outside. Scott motioned Joey into her office and directed her to sit. She finished giving instructions via a two-way radio and then turned to Joey.

"So how's Christian doing?" Scott asked.

Joey took a deep breath. "I really don't know," she answered. "I haven't seen him at school, and he isn't answering my calls or texts."

"You think he's okay?"

"I'm not sure. I can't imagine going through what he's going through right now. And I'm not sure there's any rational way to respond to something like this. But I get the feeling he's ready to explode."

"Explode?"

"Yes—and I don't know what that'll look like. I'm trying to be there to listen if he needs someone to talk to. But he's pushing me away. And I'm afraid he's going to do something."

"Do what?"

Joey shook her head. "Sebastian, the guy who was killed, was like a brother to Christian. Kenzie, his cousin, was like his big sister. They're really the only family he has. I don't know what his life looks like without them. I know it's not pretty. I get the impression that they were the people standing between him and the streets when he was in high school. That they were responsible for directing him onto the right path."

Mrs. Scott looked into Joey's eyes and clutched her hand. "I want you to call me if you need anything," she directed. "Call me if there's anything I can do for Christian. Or you. Anything."

"I don't know what to do."

"You're doing the best thing—making yourself available if he needs you. Follow your instincts. It may not seem like he wants your help. But inside, he's probably screaming for it."

Chapter 58

Sebastian's casket sat behind his excavated plot under a tent surrounded by a sea of flowers. As mourners gathered around the tent, an ambulance slowly made its way to the burial site, lights flashings, sirens off. The ambulance stopped short of the tent. Two men went to the back of the vehicle, opened its door, and lowered Kenzie down in a wheelchair. One of the men carried the oxygen tank connected by tubing to her nose. They wheeled her to the casket and then draped a large blanket around her. Three men in military uniforms walked to the front of the tent. Two saluted. The third lifted his trumpet and began playing. When the trumpeter finished, a woman dressed in a black dress moved into place and began singing.

"Why should I be dis-cour-aged and why should the shad-ows come," she sang.

Maddie stood frozen like a statue with Daija and Cordell to either side of her. She prayed silently that Kenzie would fully recover, regain her ability to walk and talk. How could Maddie possibly care for these children at her age? She took a deep breath and focused on the soloist.

"When Je-sus is my por-tion," she sang. "A con-stant Friend is He. His eye is on the spar-row, and I know that he watch-es me."

Christian closed his eyes and tried to summon the strength he'd need. Fate had delivered a job to his doorstep. It may well be the last job he'd ever do. Who was he to turn it down?

He looked at Kenzie, and then at Daija and Cordell. He silently prayed that he'd see them again after tonight. But he couldn't think about that now.

He distracted himself by mouthing the words the soloist sang.

"I sing be-cause I'm hap-py! I sing be-cause I'm free! For His eye is on the spar-row, and I know He watch-es me."

Joey could barely see through the tears clouding her eyes. She hated the utter senselessness of the killing, grieved for a wife who'd lost her husband, children who'd lost their father and were at the same time losing their mother, felt a pain that made it all feel too personal. Even as Kenzie improved, it was doubtful that she'd ever be the same.

As the soloist finished and mourners consoled each other, Joey wiped the tears from her eyes as she spotted

Christian in the distance speaking with a young man she'd never seen before.

"This is for you," Deante said, handing a brown paper bag to Christian.

Christian tucked the bag into his jacket. "Thanks."

"I'll see you later," D-man said.

"Later," Christian said.

Chapter 59

Christian walked purposely to his car in FDU's student parking lot. One of the lights in the parking lot flickered off and on, and a second wasn't working. Still, the lights from the campus buildings in the distance provided some illumination. He spotted someone sitting on his hood, but didn't realize it was Joey until he got closer.

"What are you doing?" he asked.

"Waiting for you," she replied.

"Why?"

She hugged him. He stood motionless. "I'm thinking about you. Praying for your family," she said. "And I'm here for you if you need to talk."

"Thanks," he said. "I really need to get going."

She didn't move from the hood. "Where is it?" she asked.

"What?"

"Whatever that young man gave you at the funeral."

"I don't know what you're talking about," he muttered. "But as I said, I've got to go. So if you don't mind."

She got off the hood. She patted the outside of his jacket and felt a hard object on his side. "What's that?" she asked. "Is it what I think it is?"

He gently pushed her hand aside. "It's nothing," he told her.

"Then let me see."

"No."

She stood in front of the driver's side door. "I'm not leaving until I see it."

"If I show you, will you leave?"

She nodded. He hiked his jacket upward. Strapped to his side was a small black handgun.

"Are you crazy?" she asked. "What are you planning to do with that?"

"Handle my business," he said, softly. "Friend of mine, guy who was also shot at the barbershop—he's identified who's responsible, and where we can find him tonight."

"Have you called the police and told them?"

"That's a joke, right?"

"What are you going to do?"

He shrugged his shoulders. "Listen," he instructed. "I appreciate everything you've done. You're a good person. A good friend, actually. But I have to do what I have to do. I need to make this right. Stand up for my family."

She moved aside. "So you're going to just throw your life away?"

He turned toward her. "For someone who has survived twenty-one years of life, you really don't understand a lot about the streets," he said.

"School me," she urged.

"You can't always rely on others to make things right," he noted. "Some things you have to handle on your own."

"You ever think that I've survived this long because I've stayed away from the streets?" she asked.

He opened the car door.

"And what about Daija and Cordell?" she asked.

"What about them?"

"How you going to help them if you're shot or killed? They need you now more than ever. Can't you see that?"

"You don't understand," he said. "You think the police care about some niggers who got shot in the hood? By a gangbanger? You think anyone will make this right if we don't?" He threw his hands in the air. "What do you want me to do—go create one of them ghetto memorials like the one outside the barbershop with empty liquor bottles and fake flowers?"

She opened her arms wide as she tried to prevent her tears. "Guess I can't stop you. Come say goodbye," she requested. "And make me one promise."

"What?"

"That you'll at least go say goodbye to Maddie and the kids. Before you go do what you think you have to do."

He slipped comfortably into her arms, tried not to look straight into her eyes, but he couldn't stop the tears that had begun flowing. He enjoyed the scent of her perfume.

He suddenly began shivering uncontrollably, felt powerless to hold himself up, and began falling to his knees. As she embraced him, the vibrations from his shivering left his body and flowed through hers. It created a sort of electricity that temporarily bound them.

"You don't have to do this," she said. "Please don't do this. I'm begging you. Just stay with me."

He couldn't do this. He needed to get on the bus and watch from a safe distance as that officer had once instructed. The streets were indeed calling his name, but he no longer possessed the skills or street sense to survive that way of life. It had become foreign to him.

ↄ✺ↄ

Wrapped in a blanket, Joey sat on the hallway floor outside Christian's dorm room. She huddled close enough to the door that she could feel the heat emanating from his room, and she wondered what she'd do if the door sprang open and he emerged. There was no way she could physically stop him if he decided to venture into the streets with Deante.

Without a doubt, she'd felt something special as she'd held Christian in her arms in the parking lot. Was what she felt that special feeling her mother and others had always told her about? Since childhood, she'd been told that there was one special person for her—someone with whom she was fated to be, and that she'd recognize the person by the unique feeling created by his touch, a touch like she'd never experienced before and would never experience with anyone else. A silly wives' tale, she'd always thought

She had no idea if what she'd felt in the parking lot was that special feeling. Perhaps her mother would know for sure. But she'd never find out if it was or wasn't if Christian left his room with that gun. Getting him back to the room was one job—getting him to get rid of that gun would be the next.

❧❧

Inside the room, Christian sat on his bed staring at the small handgun resting on his desk. It was shiny, with defined angles, aesthetically pleasing for something designed to injure, maim, and kill. He tried again to summon the strength he'd need to kill, to avenge the murder of Sebastian and the maiming of Kenzie. He couldn't comprehend what would be worse—going out and killing or forever living with the realization that he couldn't.

Chapter 60

Tobias breathed slowly, deliberately, as he opened his eyes and viewed his surroundings—the late afternoon sunlight filtering in from the lone window in his hospital room, which produced a fire color on the pole holding his IV bag, the hodgepodge of items on the tray hovering near his bed, and the monitor connected to one of his fingers that continuously measured his heart rate. On the other side of his bed, Donna sat silently in the one chair on his side of the shared room.

"When'd you get here?" he asked.

"About twenty minutes ago."

"Why didn't you wake me?"

She smiled instead of answering directly. "How are you doing?"

"Been better," he replied. "But I'm feeling better today than I felt yesterday. Better than I felt last week. And they're telling me that I can get out of here as soon as I learn a few more things."

"That's great to hear, Mr. Winslow. I'm so sorry this happened to you, but I'm so glad you're pulling through it. I've been praying for you."

"Thanks."

He pointed to a small table next to Donna. "Can you please hand me that washcloth?"

"Sure."

He wet the cloth with water from the small plastic pitcher on his tray and then wiped his face. "There's a few things I wanted to do at my apartment before Lakisha arrives. To make things a little nicer until we can move into that house I told you about on the phone."

"Actually, that's why I'm here," Donna said. "Considering all that's happened, it would probably be best if we put off Lakisha's arrival."

"Put it off? Why?"

"You need to focus on yourself right now. Get out of the hospital and through rehab and establish a routine for yourself before we introduce Lakisha into the picture. At least that's what I going to recommend in my report."

"Wish you wouldn't do that," he said. "I'll be out of here in a couple of days."

"Yes, but how are you going to take care of yourself? I'm not talking about canceling the move, rather postponing it."

"Please let me think for a second," he requested.

He remembered what Donna's former colleague, Eric Washington, had told him; that Lakisha wouldn't survive in LA, and that the best thing he could do for her was put distance between the girl and her West Coast family. Up until this point in his life, Tobias's biggest accomplishment had been not returning to prison after his release and somehow managing to stay below the radar. Cutting hair five days a week was never going to get him into any *Who's Who* book, but it was an honest living and would enable him to provide for his granddaughter. Postponing her arrival would only give him more time to doubt he could do this, and he'd already decided he had to do this. He hadn't chosen this job. It chose him. He had failed in some many other areas of his life. He needed to succeed this time.

"What day is this?" he asked.

"Friday," Donna answered.

"So you're not going to put your report into until Monday—when you get back to LA?"

"Probably."

Tobias reached over and grasped her hand. "Do me a favor?"

"Maybe."

"Don't file the report 'til the end of next week."

∽∽∽

"Okay. We're going to try to make it a little farther today, Mrs. Frazier. See if we can do better today than yesterday."

At the rehabilitation center in Westlake, Kenzie used her arms to prop herself up inside two, long parallel bars.

One aide stood on one side of the bars. Another stood on the other side, guiding the portable oxygen machine that was attached by tubes to the mask hovering over Kenzie's face, to make sure the tubes didn't get entangled.

On the other end of the gym, aides helped other patients navigate a shallow pool. In the middle of the room, other patients sat on mats and exercised with kettle bells. Others went from station to station on a weight machine. Above the spacious room in an enclosed landing, Maddie peered below.

"You ready?" one of the aides asked.

Kenzie nodded.

"Okay. Let's start."

Kenzie slowly lifted her right leg up and then down onto the padded mat under her feet, sliding her arm forward along the bar as she did. She grimaced in pain as her foot gently landed on the mat.

"Okay," the aide said. "Your left now."

Kenzie started to move her other leg.

Maddie looked away. She could barely stand to watch. It was excruciating to see her once active daughter struggle to walk. Maddie smiled as she recalled the episode, years earlier, when her husband took Kenzie to the park to teach her to ride her bicycle without training wheels.

Maddie hadn't even had time to fix herself a cup of tea or to start dinner before they'd returned home.

"Back so soon?" Maddie asked her husband when he came through the front door. "Where's Kenzie?"

He pointed outside. Training wheels removed, Kenzie was racing up and down the driveway and around the house on her bike—

"Mrs. Dubois?"

A well-dressed man carrying a briefcase entered the room overlooking the gym. Maddie looked away from the gym as the man opened his attaché case.

"They told me downstairs that I could find you up here," he said, extending his hand. "I'm Phillip Harris. We spoke on the phone."

Harris was Sebastian and Kenzie's business manager. With Sebastian dead and Kenzie disabled, Maddie had retained power-of-attorney to oversee their business affairs until her daughter recovered.

"Oh, yes," Maddie acknowledged. "Thank you for meeting me here."

"No problem," he said. "I'm sorry we have to meet under such circumstances. But as I mentioned on the phone, there are a few legal matters we have to address."

"Yes, of course," Maddie answered.

He slid a document and a pen over to her.

"What's this?"

"This one's for the insurance company," Harris said. "The insurance on the restaurant will continue to pay the employees, up to six months, until the place either reopens or they find new jobs. But that process won't start until we get the paperwork in." He pointed to the paper. "I need you to sign and date this."

"Okay."

"The other pressing matter is the perishable foods at the restaurant," he continued. "The boxes in the walk-in freezer, at least those that haven't been opened, can be returned to the supplier for a credit. If you'd like."

"Fine," she said.

"The other stuff—the refrigerated things that will go bad, I'll put in the dumpster."

Maddie looked down at the gym and then back at Harris. "Can any of that go to a food bank?"

He nodded in agreement. "I guess. I don't see why not. I'll make a couple of calls." Harris stood. "That's all for now," he said. "I'll get this over to the insurance company right away. I'll call you once the other things are handled."

"Thank you, Mr. Harris."

Downstairs, in the gym, Kenzie had made her way halfway through the parallel bars.

"Do you need to take a break?" one of the aides asked.

"No," Kenzie said, softly. "Let's keep going."

"Okay."

Maddie fought back tears as she watched Kenzie. Truth be told, her daughter had been her main inspiration following her husband's death more than a decade prior. And it was Kenzie who had motivated Maddie to start the Wilfred Foster Society. After hearing her mother speak one day at a library in Louisiana, Kenzie climbed into her mother's lap later that evening.

"Mom?" she asked.

"Yes?"

"Who's gonna make sure that they never stop looking for that boy?"

"What boy?" Maddie asked.

"Wilfred," Kenzie responded. "The one who disappeared. His mother must be real sad."

Chapter 61

Now it's your turn."

The diabetes educator sat the doll and needle on the table next to Tobias's hospital bed. She then removed the plastic, pretend food items from the plate on the tray, and put the insulin dosing instructions on the table. She handed the doll to Tobias. It was made of cushy material and was red, except for the several areas of its body that were highlighted in yellow.

"Let's start with injections," she instructed. "I want you to inject this doll as if you were injecting yourself."

Tobias picked up the doll. He jammed the needle into the doll's head, and then he applied pressure to the push button at the top of the needle until it stopped.

"Is that where you'd inject yourself, Mr. Winslow?" she asked.

He exhaled.

"Then do it again," she directed. "This time, the right way. I can tell you that your doctor is not going to discharge you until he or she is confident you understand this—based on my recommendation."

He held the doll in one hand and with the other guided the needle into one of the areas highlighted in yellow on the doll's body.

"That's good," she said. "It's important that you inject in the right areas. Never directly into a muscle. Understand?"

"Yes."

"Also, if the last time you injected was in one area, then try another area for the next injection. You don't want to always inject in the same area. It can cause callousness below the skin."

"Okay."

She pulled the doll and needle from the tray and pushed the plate and the food items forward.

"Okay," she continued. "You're going to pretend that this is a meal you're planning. I want you to put together a meal that has an acceptable amount of proteins and carbs."

He looked at the pretend items. "What's this?" he asked, pointing to a brown object that was round.

"Let's say it's a steak. And that item next to it is a cheeseburger."

"Okay."

He placed the pretend steak on the plate. Then he stared at the vegetable choices and put asparagus on the plate.

"Good," she said. "What else?"

He put a baked potato and two rolls on the plate.

"Anything to drink?" she asked.

He placed an empty can of regular soda by the plate. She looked over his work.

"Have you been reading the materials that I gave you on carb values, Mr. Winslow?"

He didn't answer.

"The steak and vegetables are good choices," she said. "But you wouldn't want both the baked potato and the bread. Way too many carbs. Possibly you'd have a baked potato this time. Next meal, maybe a small piece of bread. And I'd encourage you to find something other than pop to drink. It adds absolutely no nutritional value. Think of it as sugar in water."

"Been drinking soda all my life," he confided.

"And you're sitting in a hospital with abnormally high blood sugar—an insulin drip connected to you for the past week. What docs that tell you?"

He didn't answer.

"Mr. Winslow, you get as many carbs in that one soda as you should have for an entire meal. If you must drink soda, try diet. A much better idea would be water or those flavored waters with no sugar."

He sighed. "You saying I can't have potatoes, bread, or soda?"

"I didn't say that. It's not about banning certain foods," she explained. "If I told you to do that, you wouldn't be able to. You'd get frustrated and stop trying. No, it's about moderation and making better choices each day. You need to go from living to eat to eating to live."

"You've lost me."

"Let's say you're at a fast food restaurant."

"Okay."

"Not that you want to be constantly at those places. But let's say one day you're away from home and it's just easy to stop by one."

"Sure."

"Well, say you order a cheeseburger and fries. A small fry. Then, you skip the soda, drink water, or get diet. The bun's a carb, the fries are a carb, and the regular soda would be one. Understanding that, you decide to spend your carb allowance on two of the three."

"I'm never gonna remember all of this," he fretted.

"Don't have to," she replied. "As much as you can, plan your meals ahead of time. And you can take this booklet wherever you go. Okay, let's go over the insulin dosage routine one more time."

"Okay."

"So what are you taking at night?"

He pointed to the insulin pen.

"Yes," she affirmed. "The doctor will set your daily dosage. You'll take this once daily. It's the long-acting insulin. Let's say you've tested right before lunch. Your blood glucose was one hundred fifteen. What do you do?"

"Take some of this one?" he asked, pointing to the small insulin vial.

"One hundred fifteen," she repeated.

He glanced at the chart in his booklet. "Guess I wouldn't take any at all. According to this."

"Yes," she said. "The fast-acting insulin is used to adjust levels throughout the day. So what if the meter read one hundred sixty-three?"

He read the chart again. "Mmm," he pondered. "Looks like I'd need four units."

"Of what?"

"The fast-acting stuff?"

"Yes, that's right," she confirmed. "We're getting there, Mr. Winslow."

Chapter 62

At one end of the FDU student center, dozens of students cheered as they watched a football game. Other students stood in lines at the various food vendors. Some had moved tables together and played board games. Despite the ruckus and Joey sitting across from him, Christian felt alone as he sat at a table in the middle of the room.

"I'm so proud of you," Joey said.

Christian didn't immediately respond to Joey's proclamation. Instead, he focused on the books spread in front of him. "Why are you proud of me?" he finally asked. "I didn't do anything."

"That's why," she answered. "The police have arrested the shooter. The newspaper says he's already confessed. And Kenzie's improving."

"None of that's going to bring Sebastian back. Or get rid of this feeling I have."

"What feeling is that?"

"Cowardice."

"Don't be silly. You're not a coward," she said. "You're a survivor."

"You don't get it, do you?" he asked.

"No, I guess I don't."

"That animal doesn't deserve to live. He doesn't deserve to breathe the same air that we do."

"Probably not," she agreed. "But only God gets to make that call."

"I should've made the call," he insisted. "But I let you talk me out of it. Now, I'll have to live with that for the rest of my life."

She took a deep breath. "I'm glad you didn't do anything," she said. "And I can deal with you being upset with me. I'm sure your Aunt Maddie, Daija, Cordell, and Kenzie would be glad too if they had any idea what you planned on doing."

"Why's that?"

"Because they don't need you to *die* for them," she reasoned. "They need you to *live* for them." She reached across the table and grasped his hand. "Can I ask you something?"

He grinned. "Is there any point in me trying to stop you from asking?"

She playfully slapped his hand. "The other night, by the car," she began. "Did you feel anything special?"

"Special?"

"In your body?"

"I felt anger. Rage," he recalled. "The strong urge to kill."

"Was that it?"

"No," he confided. "Felt pain too. Still feel pain."

Chapter 63

Tobias glanced at the clock on the wall in the hospital room and then back over to the small television near the end of his bed. He'd been watching one of the cable news channels. But as he was into the second hour of viewing, the channel was now repeating the same stories. After a moment or two, he pressed the call button next to his bed.

"Yes, Mr. Winslow?" a nurse said through the intercom.

"What time you 'spect that doctor to be here?" Tobias asked.

"Mr. Winslow, I believe he's in the hospital making his rounds. I'm sure he'll get to you before long. Is there anything I can do for you?"

"The nurse 'fore you said I can't leave until I see the doctor," he informed her. "And I really need to be getting outta here."

"I'll page him, Mr. Winslow."

"Thanks. Don't mean to be a bother."

"It's no problem."

Tobias got out of the bed. He'd already taken off his hospital gown and put on the jeans and sweatshirt Cameron had brought. He walked out to the nurses' station and got a plastic garbage bag. Back in his room, he packed his things into the bag, including the booklets and various forms he'd signed and the prescriptions he needed to fill. The patient in the bed next to him couldn't speak, so Tobias stared out the small window in the room.

In the distance, he saw the RTA train making its way west to the airport. He thought about all the things he still needed to do before Lakisha arrived. He'd cleaned the room where she'd stayed weeks ago, but he'd still hoped to rent a carpet shampooer from the grocery store and replace the shower curtain in the bathroom.

He couldn't do any of that in the hospital room. He also worried about the barbershop. Had Cameron replaced the broken plate glass with wood or gotten someone to replace it? He shouldn't have been worrying about his shop. That would take care of itself. But he wanted the apartment to look good when Lakisha and the people from social services arrived.

He was sorting through different scenarios when the doctor finally came in. He retrieved the chart near the door and began reading it. "Understand you've been looking for me, Mr. Winslow."

"Yes, Doctor," Tobias replied. "They tell me I can't get outta this place until you say so."

"That's usually how it works," the doctor replied. "Guess that's why they pay me the big bucks. Your blood glucose levels look good. You've kept them at acceptable levels for two days now. How are you feeling strength-wise?"

"I'm getting there," Tobias proclaimed. "I've been able to get up, move around, walk around the floor. Got a little dizzy a couple of times, but then it stopped. Haven't needed the walker."

"Good. Exercise is good," the doctor said. "Tell me about your insulin regime."

"Well, I've got two different kinds. I'm supposed to test in the morning, before meals, and at bedtime. Depending on what the meter says, I may have to inject some insulin."

"Which one is that?"

Tobias shuffled through the plastic bag and pulled out the small vial. "This one," he said, holding out the vial.

"And what about the other one?"

"I take that one once a day. At night. Can I go now?"

"Mr. Winslow, I'm a little concerned that you're going straight home instead of to a rehab facility. You do seem to be doing well. But I'd feel more comfortable if you were somewhere where you were being monitored, in case there's a setback."

"Doc, the best rehab I can get will be at home and my job," Tobias assured him. "No point in staying here and having folks telling me the same things over and over. I get it. I'm sure there are other folks who need the bed."

"Okay," the doctor conceded. "But I want you to meet with a hospital social worker before you're discharged. They'll go over all the different resources available. You're ready to get back home. I get that. But we don't want to see you back here in a couple of weeks. That wouldn't be good for anybody. I'll call down and have someone come up."

"Thanks for everything," Tobias said. "Appreciate it, Doc."

The doctor extended his hand. "Good luck, Mr. Winslow."

Chapter 64

The crowd gathered outside Kenzie's house clapped and cheered as an ambulance pulled into her driveway. A "welcome home" banner hung over the front door, and several television crews recorded the scene from the street. A wheelchair was brought to the van, but Kenzie waved it off and called for a walker instead. An aide helped her step out of the van.

"Mrs. Frazier, can we have a few words?" one of the reporters shouted.

Kenzie motioned the television crews forward, but Maddie quickly positioned herself between Kenzie and the reporters. "My daughter is very weak," she said. "Perhaps she can make a brief statement. But there'll be no questions."

The reporters stuck their microphones in front of Kenzie's face.

"Thank you. Thank you for all of your prayers,"

Kenzie said, slowly. "Please keep praying for me and my family."

Maddie stepped in. "Thanks for coming," she said. "That'll be all."

The reporters shouted questions as the aide helped Kenzie inside the house and into the bedroom that had been prepared for her. The guests inside helped themselves to the food that neighbors and friends had been delivering to the house for weeks.

Joey stared out a window. Christian eased behind her, placing his arms around her waist. She closed her eyes and allowed herself to relax into his arms. She enjoyed the scent of his cologne.

"I don't know how I'm going to get through all of this without you," he said.

"I'm not going anywhere," she assured him.

He kissed her lightly on the back of her head. She turned toward him.

"I'm going home in a few days," she announced, smiling.

"Where?" he asked.

"Houston."

"Good," he replied. "Lord knows you need a break. And I'm sure you'll have a good time with your family."

"I'd like you to come with me," she said. "I want you to meet my mother."

"You would?"

"Yes. And a couple days away would do you some good as well. One of my uncles works for the airline, so I can get you a really cheap ticket."

"How cheap?"

"It wasn't that much."

"Do I have a choice?"

She smiled.

୧୬୧

Marcel was the first to arrive at the barbershop on Tuesday. But by the time he'd gotten out of his car and hobbled to the door on his crutches, Cameron had parked in the small lot behind the shop and was unlocking the front security gate. There were three parking spots behind the shop—reserved for Tobias, Cameron, and Chante. Not knowing when Tobias would return, Marcel thought better of parking in his spot.

"Is it Tuesday already?" Marcel asked. He snapped his fingers. "Seems like my weekend came and went like that."

Cameron glanced at Marcel's bandaged leg. "How ya feeling?"

"Some days are better than others," Marcel commented. "Hard to sleep while I'm thinking 'bout accidentally rolling over on the leg. And the few times I have rolled over on it, talk about pain."

"They give you something to take?"

"Yeah, they did. But they say that stuff is addictive. That people start on it and then go to heroin. That's scary. I'd rather stick with the ice on and off every thirty minutes and Tylenol."

Cameron shook his head. "Don't be 'fraid to take it if

you need it. That's what it's for. You can't control what these addicts and junkies do."

"Yeah, but I don't wanna become one of 'em."

Cameron turned on the lights as they entered the shop. Marcel made his way over to his station, dropped his bag on his seat, and took off his coat. Cameron grabbed Marcel's coat and hung it on the coat rack.

"Thanks," Marcel said.

He then reached for the outdoor broom and dustpan.

"What you doing?" Marcel asked.

"It's Tuesday," Cameron retorted. "Sidewalk needs to be swept."

Marcel reached for his crutches. "I can do that."

Cameron held out his hand. "No, no," he instructed. "I'll handle it today."

Outside, Cameron set the broom and dustpan down near the front door. Then he walked to his car behind the shop and retrieved a large box from his trunk. Back out front, he collected the stuffed animals, liquor bottles, cards, and flowers on the sidewalk along the shop and put them into the box. He tossed the box in the dumpster. The journalists and the people driving by all day to see the place where it all happened would have to fixate on something else.

As he swept the sidewalk in front of the business, the owner of the convenience store down the block approached.

"Good morning," the shopkeeper said in greeting.

"Morning."

Ahmad. Mohammed. Cameron didn't remember the

man's name. And neither Tobias nor Chante were around to refresh his memory.

"How's Mr. Winslow?" the man inquired.

"He's hanging in there. He's gonna be okay. He's dealing with a lot of issues right now. Probably won't be in for a couple of weeks."

The shopkeeper smiled. "Every day, 'bout eleven-fifteen, I expect to see him coming through the door for his smokes and large Coke. I already have them up on the counter 'fore he arrives."

Cameron laughed. "Don't know if he's gonna be buying too many more smokes. And he'll probably have to make that a Diet Coke."

The shopkeeper laughed. "Life," he said. "Please tell Tobias I said hello. Tell him I'm praying for him."

"Will do."

Cameron finished sweeping the sidewalk and went back into the shop. He put the broom and dustpan away but stood in the entranceway when he spotted Deante turn the corner toward the shop. He blocked Deante's path when he attempted to enter.

"Where 'ya going?" he asked the young man.

"Inside. To rap with Marcel. Something wrong, Mr. Maddox?"

"Yeah, there's something wrong, all right. Some lowlife took an automatic weapon and fired into our shop. Killed a good man, injured several others."

"You saying that's my fault?"

"No, Deante, that's not your fault," Cameron said. "They arrested the one responsible."

"Then what's the problem?"

Cameron took a deep breath. "There's an old saying," he stated. "If you lie down with dogs, you'll get up with fleas?"

"Huh?"

"You're not welcome here anymore. Take your business elsewhere. Come back again, and I'll have to call the law."

Chapter 65

*S*ome dressed in robes, others in pajamas, a steady line of women made their way down the cafeteria line. They moved from station to station like products on an assembly line, stopping only momentarily to indicate they'd welcome a portion of the item in front of them on their plates.

Vernita hovered near the Salisbury steak and then again near the corn and the fruit cocktail. She paused briefly in front of the applesauce but then resumed her movement before the server could extend a large spoonful.

The line came to halt when she hovered near the drink station. Vernita looked straight forward as she held her tray and slowly, methodically, mouthed inaudible words.

"Thank you," she said silently. "Thank you."

Tears flowed from her eyes as an aide motioned her to move along.

"Thank you," she said softly and silently. "You done good by Willie."

⌘

Chante shook Tobias until he awoke. He looked up from her passenger seat out across the airport parking garage. Then he took a deep breath.

"Here already?" he said.

"Yes," Chante answered. "You okay?

He nodded.

"I told you I could've picked Lakisha up and brought her to your place. You should be in bed resting."

He opened the passenger door, careful not to hit the car wedged into the adjoining parking spot. "Think you could've parked any closer to this car?" he asked, sarcastically.

She didn't answer. Instead, she looked at the directional signs posted throughout the garage, down at her cellphone, and then opened the driver's side door. "We need to go this way," she directed, pointing to the elevator entrance. "I haven't gotten an alert saying the flight has arrived. We've still got time."

They made their way to the elevator and then across the skywalk to the main terminal. He lumbered a step or two behind her. She stopped several times to allow him to catch up. She wasn't sure if his slow pace was due to a lack of strength or his anxiousness of what was to come.

"You sure you okay?" she asked. "You're not looking so good. I'll get a wheelchair once we get in the terminal."

"Don't need no wheelchair," he grumbled.

"Okay. Why don't we find a bench when we get over there and sit down for a bit?"

"Let's get to baggage claim," he suggested. "Then I can step outside for a bit of fresh air."

As they approached the escalator to the baggage claim, Chante gently pulled Tobias aside as Christian and Joey raced past them. Christian accidentally nudged Chante with one of his bags.

"Excuse me. My bad," Christian apologized, stopping briefly as he and Joey raced toward the security line.

He urged Joey to pick up the pace.

"I told you we should've left earlier!" he said. "I hope we can get through this TSA line and to the gate in time."

"Sorry!" she said.

Chante and Tobias went down the escalator to the baggage claim. They stepped outside, and he eased down onto a bench. He reached into his jacket and pulled out a cigarette.

"Really?" Chante asked. She snatched it from him. "You don't see any of these no-smoking signs everywhere? Let me be clear, if I'm going to be part of this team, it's going to be a no-smoking team. And you're going to take your medicine and visit the doctor regularly."

"Yes, Mother," he said.

"Didn't the doctors at the hospital talk to you about

that? It's a horrible example for Lakisha."

He shook his head. "You're right," he agreed. "You're right. Let's go back in."

Inside, Chante looked at the flight board and saw that Lakisha's plane had landed and was heading to the gate. "They'll be here in a few minutes," she said. "You ready?"

"Ready as ever," he replied.

೮৯೮৯

In the waiting area next to their gate, Christian reached across his seat and held Joey's hand.

"There's something I need to tell you," he disclosed. "I haven't been completely honest with you."

"What do you mean?" she asked.

"That night in the parking lot, by my car, I did feel something. But I have no idea how to describe it," he admitted.

"Go on."

"This is going to sound crazy. And please don't laugh. When you were holding me, I could feel your heartbeat racing through me, as if my own was no longer there. There was just one. Scared the hell out of me. Does that sound silly?"

She smiled. "No."

"I'm not sure what frightened me more," he continued. "That strange feeling coming from you or that thing I wanted to do. But it was that feeling that made me pause, forced me to go back to my room. I had to figure it out."

"Thank you for sharing that," she said.

He reached into the small purse on her lap and retrieved her passport. "Josephine Wilfreda Breaux," he read aloud. "Wilfreda?"

"I was named for a relative," she told him. "Let me see yours."

He handed her his driver's license.

"Christian Addison Taylor," she read. "Addison?"

"Distant aunt. Never met her," he said. "This friendship, or whatever it is—it was a long time in the making."

"Indeed it was," she agreed. "I really needed to find out who you are. Someone who adores his family. Someone working hard to better himself. Or someone willing to settle a dispute with a gun."

He smiled. "You needed to find out who *I* am?" he asked. "Not the other way around?"

"And don't get me started about those peculiar political views of yours," she continued. "And, by the way, please, please don't bring that up with my mother."

"I won't," he promised, smiling. "So what did you find out? About me?"

She smiled. "That I want to find out more."

Chapter 66

About forty miles east of Huntington, West Virginia, in a small room on the second floor of a public library, fifteen or so people sat in uncomfortable folding chairs staring at a screen on the wall. One of them, a middle-aged woman, fiddled with the projector she hoped would beam the image from her laptop unto the screen. She had already switched the power cord between the laptop and the projector twice. When she was finally able to get a clear image, the slide on the screen displayed the words "Wilfred Dreamer Event"—and everyone in the room waited for the video feed to begin.

The folks at the library stopped talking amongst themselves when Madeline Dubois appeared on the screen. Maddie smiled as she anticipated the signal from the camera operator to begin speaking. Out of view of those watching the video feed, a young woman counted down with her fingers.

"Good evening," Maddie began. "I'm Madeline Dubois, executive director of the Wilfred Foster Society. Thank you for joining us this evening. There are several developments that I wanted to share with you. And I thought this might be the best way of doing it. At least that's what the young folks keep telling me." Maddie reached for the glass of water in front of her and took a sip. "First, I'd like to thank all of you for your cards and prayers. We've suffered a great loss with the murder of my son-in-law, Sebastian Frazier, and the attempted murder of my daughter, McKenzie. I've since learned that another member of our Dreamer family was also injured in the shooting—a longtime business owner named Tobias Winslow. I had the pleasure of meeting him at a recent society meeting. You notice that I said 'murder' and that's the same wording we used in Sebastian's obituary, and in every interview I've done. He did not simply die, pass away, or expire. Such descriptions are inaccurate. His life was snatched away by a vicious gang-banger, an urban serial killer. One of the things we must stop doing is making excuses for or trying to justify criminal and immoral behavior, whether that be the violence that is destroying our communities or racially motivated hate crimes like the one that has brought us together. Some of these misguided young men and women have perfected killing black and brown people to an extent that would make the average Klansman envious. Some look to blame a lack of parenting or the failure of some young adults to take advantage of educational opportunities that Wilfred Foster would have literally killed for. I say don't put these people in jail—put them under the damn jail! You can probably tell by the tone of my voice that I'm angry. That's okay. I plan to turn that anger into action. I'd suggest you do the same."

One of the men at the library began peppering Maddie's speech with "amen" and "tell it like it is" until others glared at him, which was their way of asking him to shut up so they could hear Maddie speak.

"Kenzie is making great strides, but there's a long road ahead for her," Maddie continued. "I was hoping that this would be the year that I would hand over the reins of the society to her, but I guess God had other plans. But we will move forward. There are only three choices: Move forward, standstill, or go backward. That's doesn't mean I'm not looking forward to the day that I can step aside and watch you young folks take over. I can't say how much longer I have."

The video screen briefly dissolved into a letter before Maddie's face reappeared.

"I'd like to read several portions of a letter we received from the US Department of Justice this week. The entire letter has been posted on our website."

She read the letter:

"'We are writing to inform you that the Department of Justice and the Federal Bureau of Investigation recently conducted a review of the circumstances surrounding the disappearance and probable murder of Wilfred Foster on July 12, 1964. We regret to inform you that we are unable to proceed further with a federal criminal investigation of this matter because the men likely responsible for the disappearance and death of Mr. Foster are deceased. Please accept our sincere condolences on your loss.'"

Maddie took a deep breath before reading another portion of the letter. "'Sometime between July twelfth and twenty-third, 1964, an unknown person reported Mr. Foster's 1958 Buick, which he had purchased on July 6, 1964, abandoned near a bowling alley on the Vidalia-Ferriday highway. Several witnesses stated that they looked into the Buick in the days that followed. Some said that a belt was looped around the steering wheel, others that a necktie was hanging from the inside mirror. The majority said that they saw no bloodstains. One witness stated that he saw a silver-dollar-sized blood spot under the steering wheel. Mr. Foster's body was never found, and he is presumed dead, likely murdered."

Maddie sat silently for a moment. Someone out of view of the camera handed her a handkerchief.

"So what our government is telling us is that the crime they had no interest in investigating until we forced them to, now that crime cannot be solved because the delay in their interest has allowed the perpetrators to live out their lives and die in peace, to attend their son's and daughter's weddings, to enjoy their grandchildren. I guess what they're hoping is that we'll take this letter and the government's after-the-fact acknowledgement and go home, forget about Wilfred Foster. I, for one, will not do that."

The man at the library stood. "Speak!" he said. "Speak!"

Maddie continued. "That brings me to our next

agenda item. The third weekend of next October, please mark it on your calendars now. On that weekend, we will travel to Washington, DC, from all across the country. We will gather at the new African-American Museum and march from there to the Justice Department—or the Justice Denied Department, whichever you prefer. In the coming months, we will provide more information about that event.

"You see, whatever happened to Wilfred Foster was only the first crime. The second crime was the total indifference shown by local, state, and federal law enforcement, and the good folks of Concordia Parish. The third crime—and perhaps this is the most egregious—is the one committed in our history books at high schools and colleges and libraries across the country. You see, Wilfred Foster and thousands of others like him don't exist in their telling of history. But that's why it called *his-story*.

"I was listening to the national news a few weeks ago, and the newscaster described some shooting as the worst massacre in American history. Is that right? What about the East St. Louis massacre in 1917? Did that not happen? Can you simply deny the slaughter of black people? You can when you write the history books.

"When we allow *his-story* to be retold or untold, we dishonor Wilfred Foster and countless others. Wilfred will never live his dream. But we must do everything we can to make sure others can live theirs."

THE END

About the Author

Mark R. Lowery has lived throughout the country while writing and reporting for newspapers and magazines. Learn more about him at www.markrlowery.com

CPSIA information can be obtained
at www.ICGtesting.com
Printed in the USA
LVHW032223101019
633804LV00011B/608/P

9 781644 371237